DEEDS OF YOUTH

paksenarrion world chronicles II

ALSO BY ELIZABETH MOON

STANDALONE NOVELS
Speed of Dark
Remnant Population

THE DEED OF
PAKSENARRION
Sheepfarmer's Daughter
Divided Allegiance
Oath of Gold

PALADIN'S LEGACY
Oath of Fealty
Kings of the North
Echoes of Betrayal
Limits of Power
Crown of Renewal

THE LEGACY OF GIRD
Surrender None
Liar's Oath

VATTA'S WAR
Trading in Danger
*Marque and Reprisal^*
Engaging the Enemy
Command Decision
Victory Conditions

VATTA'S PEACE
Cold Welcome
Into the Fire

PLANET PIRATES
(with Anne McCaffrey)
Sassinak
Generation Warriors

THE SERRANO LEGACY
Hunting Party
Sporting Chance
Winning Colors
Once a Hero
Rules of Engagement
Change of Command
Against the Odds

SHORT STORY
COLLECTIONS
Lunar Activity
Phases
Moon Flights
Deeds of Honor
Deeds of Youth

^ UK title: *Moving Target*

Deeds of Youth

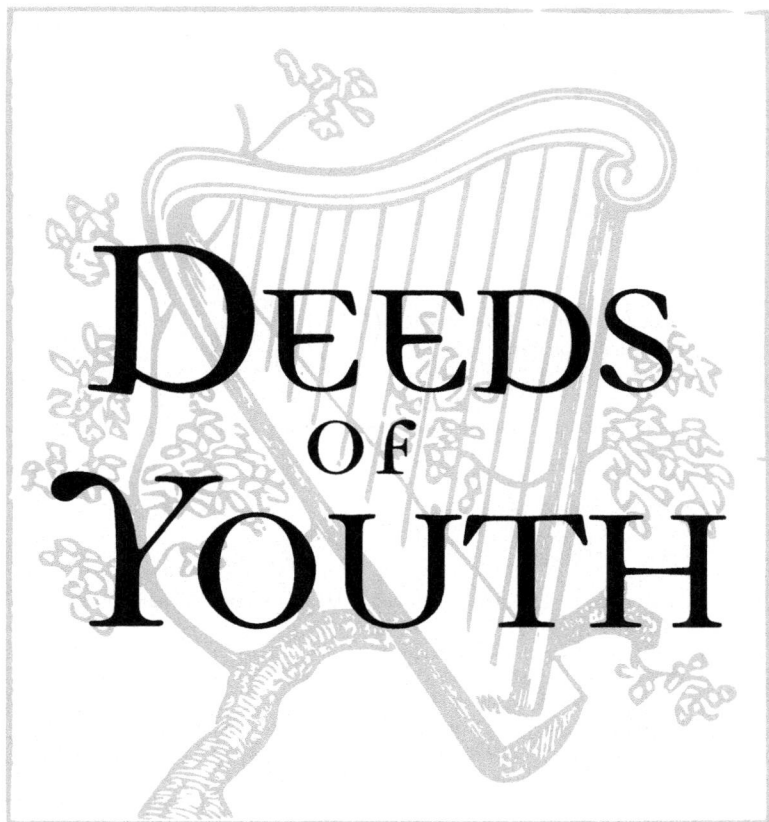

Paksenarrion World Chronicles II

Elizabeth Moon

JAB

Published by JABberwocky Literary Agency, Inc.

Collected for the first time by JABberwocky Literary Agency, Inc., in 2023.

ISBN (paperback) 978-1-625676-38-2
ISBN (ebook) 978-1-625676-37-5

Cover design by Tara O'Shea

1. "A Bad Day at Duke's East" - first published in *Deeds of Youth*. Copyright © 2023 by Elizabeth Moon.
2. "The Dun Mare's Grandchild" - early draft first published in *Paksworld Blog*, serialized, 2016. Finished for *Deeds of Youth* 2022. Copyright © 2023 by Elizabeth Moon.
3. "Dream's Quarry" - first published in *Horse Fantastic*, DAW, ed. Martin H. Greenberg & Rosalind M. Greenberg, 1991. Copyright © 1991 by Elizabeth Moon.
4. "Gifts" - first published in *Masters of Fantasy*, Baen Books, ed. Bill Fawcett & Brian Thomsen, 2004. Copyright © 2004 by Elizabeth Moon.
5. "First Blood" - first published in *Shattered Shields*, Baen Books, ed. Jennifer Brozek & Bryan Thomas Schmidt, 2014. Copyright © 2014 by Elizabeth Moon.
6. "Mercenary's Honor - first published in *Operation Arcana*, Baen Books, ed. John Joseph Adams, 2015. Copyright © 2015 by Elizabeth Moon.
7. "Consequences" - an earlier draft appeared online in Paksworld Blog, serialized, 2022. Finished for Deeds of Youth 2023. Copyright © 2023 by Elizabeth Moon.

For the latest updates about Elizabeth's novels, and everything related to *The Deed of Paksenarrion*, *Paladin's Legacy*, *The Legacy of Gird*, *Vatta's War*, and *The Serrano Legacy* series, as well as her standalone novels, visit her on the web http://www.elizabethmoon.com or the Paksworld blog www.paksworld.com/blog.

Published by JABberwocky Literary Agency, Inc.
49 W. 45th Street, Suite #5N
New York, NY 10036
awfulagent.com/ebooks

CONTENTS

Author's Note on
A Bad Day at Duke's East

Jamis Arcolin's life has changed since last summer, when he led a quiet, sheltered life in Vérella with his widowed mother and her parents. Now she's Lady Arcolin, Duke Arcolin's wife, and he's Kirgan Arcolin, the duke's heir. They live in a stronghold in northern Tsaia where he has a pony to ride, meets gnomes from his new father's tribe, horse nomads from the north, soldiers and recruits in training at the stronghold, and children of retired veterans in the nearest village. A summer's day with no lessons, a whole day to spend in the vill playing with friends? What could be better?

Publication note: "A Bad Day at Duke's East" is brand new, written exclusively for *Deeds of Youth*.

A Bad Day at Duke's East

Jamis Arcolin, mounted on his pony, smiled at the man standing on the ground waiting for a mule to be saddled.

"I know the way to Duke's East," he said. "I don't need an escort now. I know you're very busy."

"Expect you don't," the man said. Eddrin, that was, a private working for the Quartermaster through this recruit season. "But expect I'll be in trouble if I don't go with you. Orders is orders. I don't mind; it's a break from counting things."

Jamis nodded. Orders definitely were orders at Duke's Stronghold, the fort and training facility for Fox Company. Orders had been obeyed at his grandparents' home in Vérella, too, but not so quickly or—always—so thoroughly. And here he had more layers of rules and orders: his mother, his father the Duke, Captain Arneson the recruit captain, commanding here in the Duke's absence, and any adult who happened to be around. Kirgan Arcolin he might be, with the king's gift-dagger at his belt—his most treasured possession—but he was still a small boy of only seven winters.

When a groom brought the saddled mule out, Eddrin

mounted and they rode out the gate, down the road to Duke's East. Jamis took a deep breath. He had come north in the fall, after his mother's marriage to the Duke; winter had soon closed in, and though he had ridden out whenever the snow allowed, this was his first northern spring and summer. Growing up in Vérella, he had seen only a city spring—flowers appearing in the market, in window boxes, a fresher, greener smell in the air.

Near the fort, early summer grass was spangled with flowers—pink, yellow, white, and blue. Nearer Duke's East, fields of grain showed different shades of green. He could see farther than he'd ever seen before. Birds caroled around them; butterflies flitted low to the flowers. Jamis wanted to breathe in all the air in the world, with all its different smells. If not for Eddrin on the mule, he would have been tempted to kick his pony into a gallop for the feel of wind in his face.

Once past the gate to Duke's East, they rode to Mayor Fontaine's house, where the mayor's wife waved them to the stable gate. "Leave 'em here all day if you want," she said. "Heribert's over at t'mill, some need of a work crew to clean out the tailrace. I'll take care of the lad's lunch."

Behind her, two children bounced up and down. Lia and Sed, the mayor's grandchildren, and among Jamis's favorite playmates. Others were coming down the lane, having seen him ride by.

"I'll leave you to it," Eddrin said. "They'll be wanting help at the mill, no doubt. Come find me when it's time to leave, and don't wait too long."

"I'll see he remembers," the mayor's wife said.

A day free to play in the village meant a day spent running, chasing, climbing trees, gulping down a quick lunch, resting in the shade of Councilwoman Kolya's apple orchard…nothing could be better.

But the day turned out differently, all thanks to the loose latch on the mayor's piggery, which Sed had not secured in his hurry to meet Jamis. The children were hardly into a game of orcs and soldiers when Sera Fontaine found the sow rooting under the laundry she and her neighbors had spread on the village green to dry, and Sera Malander heard a noise in her pantry that turned out to be two of the piglets investigating the day's baking.

All the children were in trouble, Jamis no less than the rest. Sed blamed Jamis for his own hurry with the piggery gate; Sera Fontaine gave him a look that made him redden, though Jamis was sure it wasn't his fault. The other village children took their lead from Sed, for once, and teased Jamis about his clothes, his lack of pig-catching skills, all through the pig-catching. Soon, the others drifted off—those weren't *their* pigs—leaving all the work to Jamis, Sed, and Lia.

By the time they had the last one—squealing and squirming—back in the piggery, where the women had already herded the sow, Jamis was hot, sweaty, hungry, and dirty. Sera Fontaine scolded the three of them for getting dirty as well as being so slow to catch the piglets, and all they had for lunch was cold porridge and two-day-old bread. "Because when did I have time to fix a proper lunch today, eh?"

When they went back outside, and Jamis suggested going over to Councilwoman Kolya's apple orchard for a rest in the shade, Sed punched him in the face and called him a spoiled weakling trying to lord it over everybody when it was his fault the pigs got loose.

That did it. In moments, they were fighting, adding the lane's dust to the pigs' dirt, punching each other wherever they could. Lia screamed and joined in, pulling Jamis's hair and kicking him. Sera Fontaine came out of the house, wielding her broom; Jamis felt as if a storm had caught him up and battered him by the time she stopped. Sed had a black eye; Jamis felt like half his hair had been pulled out. His tunic was torn where Lia had yanked at it, and his nose had bled right down the front of his shirt.

"Lia, fetch me a basin of water and a rag. Sed, stand by the door and do not move. Jamis, come here." She was white-faced, her lips tight to her teeth, scary in her wrath. But she was an adult, and by the rules, he had to obey. When Lia brought the basin, Sera Fontaine swiped at the blood on his face. "You've no call to complain of Sed," she said. "Look what you did to his eye!"

"I didn't complain," Jamis said. His eyes burned with unshed tears.

"Don't talk back at me," Sera Fontaine said. "Do you want another swipe with the broom? Your father would be ashamed of you, that he would, brawling like any common brat in the street—and you as well, Sed," she said, turning on her grandson. "Your da and grandda will both have a hand on you, for this, no matter whose fault it was." She turned back to Jamis.

"You go over to the mill now and see that you tell a straight tale of what happened, start to finish. You won't be coming back to Duke's East until the mayor has had a word with your lady mother."

Jamis felt every one of the blows he'd taken as he walked off to the mill, but the worst was the way Sed and Lia looked at him. No, the worst, he thought, stumping toward the outskirts of town and the mill, was his father being ashamed of him. His father wasn't there to be ashamed, but Jamis had no doubt he would be, and that meant he had already failed at the task his father had given him as he left.

When he got to the mill, Eddrin had his boots off, his trousers rolled up, and was in the tailrace with the other men. Someone looked up, saw Jamis, and elbowed Eddrin, who looked around. His expression changed from welcoming to glowering in one instant. He climbed up onto the bank.

"What in Gird's name have you been up to?"

It wasn't my fault. Jamis bit that back. *Don't make excuses* was one rule, and *Don't lay blame on others* was another. "The pigs got loose," he said instead.

"By themselves, did they?" Eddrin said. One of the other men laughed; Eddrin shook his head. All the men had stopped working now and stared at Jamis. "Since when do pigs open latched gates by themselves?"

"You younglings been playin' in the pens again?" asked another man.

"No, sir," Jamis said. He tried to think how to tell it without laying blame on Sed, but it was Sed who'd left the latch loose. All he'd done was show up in town.

"And was it a pig gave you that bloody nose," Eddrin asked, "or was it that you got in a fight?"

"That was after," Jamis said. "After lunch. We had all caught the piglets by then, but—" He glanced at Mayor Fontaine, who had come closer still. How angry would he be? "It was after lunch," he said. "When we went outside again…"

"You thought a fight was a good way to end a day that started with letting pigs loose?" Eddrin asked. "Are you a fool, boy? Who'd you hit?"

Sed hit me first. No help for it; he had to admit they'd fought and he must not lay blame or make excuses. "Sed and I—" he said. "And then Lia—"

"Gods above, Jamis, your father would take the hide off your backside. Fighting with a girl as well as a boy? You're a disgrace— look at yourself."

Jamis looked down. Dirt all over himself, tunic torn, blood-stains on his tunic and shirt.

Eddrin turned to look at the mayor. "I'm sorry, Mayor, that I brought the brat over here or at least didn't stay with him to make sure he behaved. I'll get him home and be sure his mother will have words with him this very day."

"Boys are to trouble as bees to honey," Mayor Fontaine said. "I'm certain Sed deserves some of the blame."

Jamis looked up, hopeful, but the mayor's face was set, his lips thinned.

"Stay here and do nothing," Eddrin said, "while I fetch our mounts."

The men went back to work, ignoring Jamis. He dared not walk around or say anything, and in a short time Eddrin reappeared with the pony and the mule. He grabbed Jamis roughly and set him on the pony without ceremony, then mounted the mule and led the way to the road home. Jamis felt his eyes burning again and blinked back tears. He tried to think clearly, but his nose hurt. So did all the other places Sed or Lia had hit him. Ahead of him, Eddrin's stiff shoulders showed that he was still angry. Eddrin would tell his mother and Captain Arneson, and soon everybody at the fort would know that he, the Duke's acknowledged son and heir, had been not just foolish but stupid, careless, and rowdy, brawling in the street with the mayor's grandchildren.

He would never be allowed to visit the town again... and truthfully, he did not want to, not if it meant Sed and Lia hating him and turning the other children against him. He could imagine the sneers, the whispers, the end of all his pleasures there. He sniffed, wiped his nose on his sleeve without thinking, and made a new dirty streak. And wiping his nose made it hurt more.

* * *

When they were almost halfway to the fort, in the dip where the road couldn't be seen from the fort gate, Jamis saw a wasp settle on the mule's saddle blanket and walk back to its rump. "Look out!" he said to Eddrin. "Wasp!" He saw Eddrin turn in the saddle, and pointed to the wasp.

But the mule had already reacted, exploding into a series of bucks that sent Eddrin—unbalanced, having turned to look— right up in the air. And the mule's hind hoof kicked out sideways, caught Eddrin as he fell. He landed sprawled out, rolling, while the mule took off for the fort, and Jamis's pony shied, almost throwing him. Jamis managed to stay on, grabbing mane; when the pony finally stood still, he saw Eddrin on the ground, not moving.

"Eddrin? Are you hurt?"

No answer. Jamis looked for the mule—if it went to the stronghold, someone would come and help—but the mule had turned off the road and was rolling on the saddle. No one was in sight. No recruit cohort—it was due back some time in the next hand of days, Captain Arneson had told him. All the troops stationed at the stronghold were busy preparing for recruits to arrive, for training to begin. He saw no one when he looked back to Duke's East, either. Though he could see the very top of the gate tower, he was not at all sure a sentry there could see him from the walkway below it.

The rule for riding out was: never get off your horse between home and town unless an adult tells you to. But there were other rules: when someone is hurt, call for help. Obey the adult who is with you. Never gallop your pony toward home. Think before you act.

Jamis bit his lip, trying to think. Eddrin lay unmoving,

unspeaking, his awkward sprawl looking…wrong. One of his legs bent where it shouldn't; blood stained his trouser leg. No one was within hail, so calling for help wouldn't bring any. Riding back to town would take—half a glass at a safe pace; at a gallop it would be quicker. To the fort—but he was not supposed to gallop toward home. But it might be quicker. But Eddrin looked so helpless…and how badly was he hurt? Was he…dead?

And which rule to follow? His pony was quiet now, with the mule far enough away. Jamis looked again at Eddrin, sighed, and slipped off the pony, holding the reins firmly. He led the pony over to Eddrin, and squatted down. "Eddrin!" he said loudly. No response. Yet another rule: never touch a sleeping soldier…but he had to; he had to find out if Eddrin was…well…dead.

He reached out and shook Eddrin's shoulder. No response. Was he breathing? He couldn't tell; he put his ear down near Eddrin's open mouth. He still couldn't tell. When he looked more closely, he could see a pulse in Eddrin's neck, and when he touched it, he could feel it moving against his finger. So…maybe alive? But he couldn't pick up a grown man.

He remembered, then, how the horse nomad had sent his pony home with words that made it leap into a gallop. And his father had come. Could he do that? Would the pony understand? He tried to remember the sounds, those sounds he had heard only once. He had to do something. He tied up the reins in a knot as like the nomads' knot as he could make it, and tried out the words. His pony tossed its head and stepped aside. He tried again, louder, putting all his day's worth of misery and fear into it. The pony pinned its ears and galloped away toward the fort. They would see it when it topped the rise. He looked at Eddrin again.

Eddrin's ruddy, sunburned face had changed color; Jamis

bit his lip. It was his fault; if he hadn't said anything, Eddrin might have ridden out the buck. Tears blurred his vision, but he refused to sob. Junior yeomen did not panic and did not quit trying. That's what the Marshal said. He had to think of something— *Breathe.* Where had that thought come from, like someone speaking in his head? He took a deep breath and let it out slowly. *Breathe into him.*

Could he? Would it work? Would it make it worse? He knelt beside Eddrin, put his mouth right down on Eddrin's dry lips, and breathed into his mouth. Air came directly back at his ear, out of Eddrin's nose. That wouldn't help. Jamis pinched Eddrin's nose tight shut, then breathed into his mouth again. Nothing, though the pulse still beat in the man's neck. Had it slowed?

Breathe hard.

Jamis tried again, sucking in all the air he could, and blowing it out with all his strength. It made a sound inside Eddrin, and then it came back out his mouth with another sound, smelling different, stale and rank. Jamis tried again, sitting up to breathe in, leaning over to breathe out. Eddrin's chest moved a little. Again, harder. Once, two times, three. Then Eddrin stirred, gasped, seemed to choke, gasped again. His eyelids fluttered but did not open. Jamis let go of Eddrin's nose.

"Eddrin!" Jamis said. "Don't die!"

Eddrin groaned; his head moved a little, back and forth. A shoulder twitched. Another groan, louder this time, and a mumbled sound that might have been a word, though Jamis couldn't understand it.

"You're hurt," he said to Eddrin. "The mule bucked you off. It was a wasp."

Eddrin opened his eyes, at first vacant but then focusing on Jamis. "Wha' 'appen?"

"The mule bucked you off," Jamis said again. "Your leg's hurt."

"Go. Help."

"I sent the pony," Jamis said.

"Good." Eddrin's eyes closed again, but he kept breathing, a harsh sound in the quiet afternoon. Another wasp flew near, as if it would land on Eddrin's hair.

Jamis waved it away and then looked around. Had the pony really gone straight back to the fort? How long would it take? It felt like a long time already. There in the dip of the road, sitting on the ground, he couldn't see the fort at all. He could see the tops of the hills that now held gnomes instead of orcs. He could see the top of the ridge to the east. But nothing of Duke's East or any help coming.

He took off his tunic and laid it over Eddrin's face to keep the sun off. He considered walking up the slope toward the fort, where he could see it, but what if Eddrin stopped breathing again? He sat down, watching Eddrin's chest rise and fall, listening to his breath. It seemed a very long time, though the sun hadn't moved even a hand down the sky, when he heard hoofbeats coming from the fort. Shortly then he saw them: a tensquad, one leading his pony, the other Eddrin's mule, a pack now lashed to its saddle—poles and a roll of cloth.

"What's happened, lad?" That was Corporal Danits.

The words tumbled out of his mouth before he could sort them. "It was my fault—a wasp stung the mule and the mule bucked and if I hadn't said look for the wasp Eddrin wouldn't have been bucked off and then he wasn't breathing and I didn't know what to do—"

"He's dead, then? And you covered his face?"

"No, sir—to keep the sun out of his eyes. He's breathing now."

Danits looked at him oddly but said no more, dismounting with a nod to the others, who also dismounted. He lifted Jamis's tunic from Eddrin's face, and his expression changed from doubt to satisfaction. "He's alive after all. And with a broken leg and who knows what else. And what about you, Jamis? You've got blood all down your front—did you come off your pony?"

"No, sir. That was in Duke's East."

"Got in a fight, did you?" Danits grinned. "Happens to us all." He turned to the men. "Beldan. Ride back fast and get the surgeon. A wagon, too. Ker, rig a cloak for shade on Eddrin." He turned back to Jamis. "Now tell me what you did when Eddrin stopped breathing."

That was a hard thing, harder than talking about the fight.

"There was a voice. He said breathe."

"A voice."

"Yes. Could it have been Gird?"

"I suppose. So you breathed, and what then?"

Jamis explained as best he could. Danits' bushy eyebrows went right up his face and his mouth fell open.

"You breathed into him? And then he breathed? How long before he breathed?"

Jamis shrugged before he remembered the rule against shrugging to answer. "Sorry," he muttered. "I don't know. I was just—just trying to breathe hard enough to make his chest come up. That's all I thought about. Not many breaths."

"We'll splint the leg before we move him," Danits said to Jamis. "You know, if you hadn't breathed for him, he probably would have died."

"I—I was afraid he would. Will he get well now?"

"I expect so," Danits said. "If it's no more than a broken leg. But we'll know more when the surgeon comes. It's good you didn't try to move him. That can make things worse. But very good you breathed for him. I wouldn't have thought a boy your age would think of it."

"It was the voice," Jamis said. "That's what he said to do."

With Danits there, and the other soldiers busily unpacking the mule, and then the splinting of Eddrin's broken leg—Jamis had to swallow hard not to puke when he saw the bone ends slide back under the skin—it seemed to take less time for the surgeon to arrive, the wagon already topping the rise behind him.

"Take the lad back to the fort," the surgeon said. "He needs seeing to as well, but if he wasn't bucked off, he can ride back and his mother can clean the blood off him."

Jamis felt shaky but, once on his pony, rode back without assistance, though he had a soldier on either side. They asked no questions but whether he felt well enough to go on, and he always said yes.

His mother's reaction to his bloody nose, torn tunic, and bloodstained shirt surprised him. "Let's get you cleaned up" was all she said, and helped him off the pony, thanking the groom who led it away. Once he was inside, in the kitchen, with his mother washing the blood off his face and the cook clucking and muttering, the miseries of the day rose up like a wave and he could not stop the tears from coming.

All of it—the pigs getting loose, the difficulty of catching them all, the cold porridge for lunch, Sed hitting him, and then the chaos of the fight and Sera Fontaine's fury, then Eddrin's scolding and the miserable ride home and the wasp and the mule and Eddrin—

"Sshh," she said finally. "Try to breathe. Let's get you clean— hot water, please, Cook, for a bath upstairs. I want to be sure there's no more damage."

The bath revealed a bloody place on his scalp where some hairs had been yanked out, and bruises all over his arms and legs. His head ached; his nose was so stuffy he could hardly breathe through it, and he was tired beyond tired.

"We'll sort this out later," his mother said. She went to the cupboard and pulled out a small glass jar. "A mug of sib and honey with a few drops of this, and you'll sleep for a glass or two."

* * *

He woke in the big bed in his parents' room, with a fire crackling on the hearth. His mother sat in her favorite chair, busy with yarn and needles, the very image of safety and home. He felt vaguely sore, but nothing hurt enough to bother, and he was immediately hungry. She looked over at him.

"Better now?"

"Yes, Mother. What— Is it tomorrow?"

"No, not nearly. Are you hungry?"

He was ravenous. He pushed himself up. "Yes, Mother. Shall I get dressed?"

"No need. You can eat in your night things for once, and then I'll warm your bed in your own room and you can sleep until morning. How does a hot ham roll sound? And a mug of soup?"

Nothing more was said of his day as he ate the roll and the soup, while she and one of the servants worked across the passage in his room. Nothing was said but "Good night, sleep well" when he had used the pot and climbed into his own bed.

In the morning, he woke with no worse than a swollen nose and dressed himself before his mother came in. He had the previous day laid out in order in his mind now, and he knew he would have to tell her about it. But she would not hear it during breakfast. Instead, she told him that the surgeon had reported on Eddrin's condition, that he would be off duty for at least eight hands of days with the broken leg, that he had such a knock on the head he seemed to remember nothing for hours before the fall.

"He says you saved Eddrin's life, Jamis. That was quick thinking on your part, to breathe into his mouth—"

"I heard a voice—"

"Yes, that's what Corporal Danits said you told him. What kind of voice?"

"A man's voice. Like Grandda, maybe, but I thought maybe, it might be Gird."

"Why Gird?"

"Because of what Marshal Donag said, in Vérella, that Gird could speak to someone if there was need."

"Hmm. It might be. Well, when you've finished breakfast, it's time for your studies. Today, I think it would be good for you to write down what happened yesterday, as best you remember it. What happened that made Sed angry enough to hit you, for instance."

His heart sank and his stomach clenched; he wanted no more breakfast. He remembered it all too well, and the problem was…how could he tell the truth and not lay blame on Sed? His mother brought a stack of wax tablets and a stylus to the table, and left him to it.

Vivid as his memory of the morning was, he found it hard to organize those memories into a coherent record. Time and again he rubbed the wax flat and started again. He was still working on the sequence of catching piglets—had Mal and Gwurn left before or after the black-and-white spotted one dodged him and made it straight into someone's garden?—when his mother interrupted him.

"Sera Fontaine has come to speak with you," she said. "And Sed and Lia are with her."

"I don't want to see them," Jamis said. "I haven't finished this, and it has to be right—"

"It's a matter for Kirgan Arcolin," she said. "And you must come."

They were waiting in the small courtyard, by the well. His mother had ordered seats brought out, and one of the folding campaign tables, with a jug of sib and a plate of pastries.

"It's very kind of you," Sera Fontaine said. "But I must speak first, if you'll allow, my lady."

"Of course you may speak first," his mother said.

"I was wrong yesterday," Sera Fontaine said. "I was that flustered, with the sow having messed up everyone's laundry and my neighbors all scolding at me, that I didn't stop to think, really. It was like your lad was the same as my lad, and I should have remembered—"

"He is the same as your lad," his mother said. "I told you that the first time we came into Duke's East: he must not get airs above himself."

"He hasn't," Sera Fontaine said. "An' I've told Sed often enough, you make your manners like the young Kirgan, and you'll be better off."

Jamis darted a glance at Sed, who looked, black eye and all, as miserable as Jamis had felt. Was he being told all the time to copy Jamis? That wouldn't be fun. He hadn't liked it in the city, when he'd been told to copy his older cousin's tidiness.

"And I've told Jamis to follow Sed's lead when playing with the other boys," his mother said. Jamis heard that with amazement. That wasn't exactly what she'd said…was this one of those "useful lies" he'd heard her laugh about with Cook? His mother…

lied sometimes?

"The thing is," Sera Fontaine said, "I was wrong to blame Jamis for the pigs gettin' loose, and for gettin' dirty catchin' em. As for the fight…my man straightened Sed on that last night, he did, and Sed admitted he hit first and called Jamis names. I reckon any boy with spirit would hit back, and younglings of soldier stock get into fights, whatever we say. So, I come out instead of Heribert—Mayor Fontaine—on account of I'm the one wrong here. And Sed's here to make his own apology, blaming someone else for his own fault." She turned to Sed. "Speak your piece now, to Jamis."

"'M sorry." Sed looked down at his feet. "Shouldn't of blamed you. Shouldn't of hit you and called names."

Jamis glanced at his mother, who nodded at him. "I'm sorry the pigs got loose; I know you didn't mean to. And I'm not angry with you, and anyway, I blacked your eye." After a long silence, during which Sed looked up and, Jamis could see, was trying to think what to say next, Jamis spoke again. "I want to be friends like we were, Sed. I like you. Can we agree?" He put out his hand, palm up, the way his father did.

Sed nodded, blinking with his good eye, and stepped forward, putting his hand palm down on Jamis's. "I won't do that again," he said.

"Good," Jamis said.

"And Lia," Sera Fontaine said, with a glance at the girl.

"I'm sorry too," she said, looking straight at Jamis. "You aren't spoiled, and I was wrong to jump in and help Sed beat you up and I'm sorry I pulled out some hair and here it is so you know I won't do any bad things with it." She held out a lock of his hair.

"I knew you wouldn't do anything bad," Jamis said. He took the hair she offered and then held out his other hand again. She put her palm in his and smiled.

"Well, now," his mother said. "Let's all take a deep breath and have some refreshment."

With the sib poured, and the pastries half-eaten, and an invitation to lunch having been refused, "Because I promised to help Seri and Arin and the rest with their laundry today and just took time to come out here." Sera Fontaine turned to Jamis. "I'm glad you got home safe, Jamis, after all that. I did worry that maybe Eddrin would put a hand to you."

"Eddrin had a fall on the way back, but Jamis took care of him," his mother said before he could answer. "He's quite the hero to the men today, though I hadn't told him that yet." She reached out and ruffled his hair, and Jamis felt his face heating. He hoped she wouldn't tell the whole story right then. She didn't. But Sera Fontaine nodded, almost as if she'd heard it.

"We'd best be getting back," she said. "Just know your lad's welcome in the vill any time he wants to come."

"I do want to come," Jamis said, before his mother could answer. "But I don't want Sed to be just like me. I like Sed the way he is. I learn things from him."

"You learn to fight?" Sera Fontaine laughed and shook her head. "Well…I suppose there's no harm, if your mother doesn't see it, in you learning more than your letters and manners from her—"

"Indeed, I think it's a good idea," his mother said. "A man should know more than his mother's ways." She paused, then went on. "Would Sed and Lia like to stay here for the afternoon? I can send them with an escort later."

"Not today," Sera Fontaine said. "But another day, if you will."

"Of course," his mother said. "They're soldiers' children;

they'll like to see more of the fort, I'm sure." Jamis grinned at Sed and Lia and they both grinned back.

"Can we ride the pony?" Sed asked.

"Hush!" Sera Fontaine scowled at Sed. "You've been on a plowhorse—"

"It's not the same."

"I don't mind," Jamis said quickly. "And I'd like to ride a plowhorse sometime. We could trade."

Sera Fontaine rolled her eyes. "Boys. Well, not today, for certain. Lady Calla, you tell me when, with a day's notice if you can—"

"Of course."

"And I'll take these two home, for there's work to be done."

"And so have we," his mother said. "Fare well, with Gird's blessings on you."

"And on you."

When the visitors were out the gate, his mother turned to him. "Well done, Jamis, in all ways. But your studies are still to finish."

With a much lighter heart, Jamis found he could get all his thoughts in a row, this time, and words to express them. But his spelling, his mother murmured, still needed more attention. She wrote the correct spellings for him on a piece of slate and bade him learn them by suppertime. That was easy, in the lightness of knowing he still had friends and would see them again.

Well done indeed.

Jamis looked around before realizing the voice was in his head. That voice. Again. "Thank you, Father Gird," he said.

The End

Author's Note on The Dun Mare's Grandchild

Market towns in northern Fintha sometimes have several horse nomad families who've been exiled from their tribe. They don't fit in easily: they look different, sound different, dress different, and cling to their strange foods and habits so they even smell different. They're targeted by judicars, blamed for petty crime, ridiculed. Their children grow up not knowing the ways of their own relatives still living on the steppes. Occasionally, someone returns to the tribe—and even more rarely, a town-born child is taken in. It all depends on something no human can calculate: the choice of one horse in their herds. For a dun mare is considered the Mare of Plenty's own daughter, and her decisions stand.

Publication note: An earlier, partial version of "The Dun Mare's Grandchild" was published online in *Paksworld Blog*, 4 sections in June & July 2016, as a serial. This final version was completed in 2022.

THE DUN MARE'S GRANDCHILD

"Again?" Oktar's mother glared at him. "Bloody nose, black eye, shirt torn, a complaint from the judicar—you're a disgrace!"

"They said we were dirty stinking horse—" He paused; the word they'd used was forbidden. "—droppings," he finished.

"You should ignore them," his mother said. "They are ill-bred; you should not dirty your hands with them."

Oktar's hands, bruised and bloody as well as his nose, were at his sides, half-hidden by his long horsefolk shirt, but he knew she knew.

"Who hit first?" she asked.

"Tam Togirdsson." He touched his nose.

"And you did not duck away. And you hit him—"

"The others were already hitting me."

"Well. Come and I will clean your face."

During that painful process—for she insisted on scrubbing out every raw scratch—Oktar took no heed of her words but went on thinking how he would get back at Tam and the others. It was not his fault. It had never been his fault. He could not help having a horsefolk name, a horsefolk face, living in the neighborhood where the small group of horsefolk in this town clumped together for protection. He'd never stolen anything, but if one of the others stole a plum from a stand in the market on the way home from the grange, *he* was the one accused. He'd never lied…well, almost never…but *he* was the one called a liar if another boy wanted to make trouble. Which they mostly did.

"There," his mother said finally. His face stung with her scrubbing. "And now you will stay inside until your father comes, and he will deal with you. You are beyond a woman's strength to beat."

His father. O Mare of Plenty, if his mother would not merely switch him with the horsetail that hung behind the kitchen door…if she actually meant for his father to punish him! He counted up the days in his head. Yes. He was indeed six days past the time his father had set, and thus…

"You will polish every pot in the kitchen," his mother said. "And then the floor. And there is no supper for you until after."

* * *

Araimak Cracolnya sat in their one chair and listened to his wife's recital of Oktar's misdeeds without a change of expression. Araimak's father, Ormaktar, squatted on his heels by the fire as usual, his black eyes gleaming like those of a gnome, his clan tattoos shadowing one side of his face. When the tale was told, Araimak stared at Oktar a long moment.

"I have heard already of this from the market judicar," he said. His horsefolk accent was much stronger than Oktar's, less than Ormaktar's. "It is a bad thing you have done. It is bad for all of us, not only you, not only this hearth, but all the horsefolk hearths. Did I sire or your mother foal a wild ass, that you bray and bite and kick like one?"

Oktar glared back. "It was not my fault," he said.

"Oh? Because a few horseflies nipped you, you must attack?"

"Because I am not a coward like—" Oktar stopped, at the look on his father's face, his grandfather's face.

"Who would you name, little ass?" his grandfather said, rising effortlessly from his squat. "Who of our people?"

Oktar knew what he wanted to say, but knew he must not.

"Me, perhaps, with my withered arm, for coming here when the tribe bade me go, called me bad luck for them?" His grandfather's labored Common, mixed with horsefolk terms, was hard to follow word by word, but the meaning was clear: Granfer was angrier than Oktar had ever seen. "You think I should have fought them, bade your father fight them, the whole tribe, and branded them with *my* bad luck?" He spat at Oktar; the spit landed on Oktar's chest, an insult barely less than on his face. "You are a fool and I would say none of your sire's get, marked with the ass's stripe, but for your dam, who is blameless in this. Sometimes a foal is born wrong; maybe that is you."

"No!" His mother spoke, switching to the speech of horsefolk where Oktar could understand only one word in four, if that. Full of hissing and clicking, that tongue was, as if talking to horses. The old man answered in the same, and then his father, and then they all fell silent and looked at him, two sets of black eyes, one of shadowed green.

"It is time you met your own folk," his father said. "You have a sickness no beating will cure, but healing comes on the grass, from the Mare of Plenty and the Windsteed's clean wind in your lungs." He nodded to Oktar's mother, who slipped away and began rattling dishes and pots.

Was he to have supper after all? And no beating? He could not understand that, and his nose hurt and his black eye and the cuts and bruises on his face and chest and the foot that had been stamped on and the shins that had been kicked. He wanted very much to sit down—to lie down, even—but he could not until his father gave him leave.

Shortly, his mother came back with a mug.

"You will drink this," his father said. "There will be no demons from the town in your belly when you leave; you will go to the People as clean as we can make you."

His mother stood behind him, firm arms around his body, holding him upright and still, while his father poured the liquid down his throat. He gulped and gagged and shuddered at the taste of it and the knowledge of what it would soon accomplish.

The next morning, before dawn, he could scarcely walk— and not steadily—when his father wakened him, took him outside, and doused him with well water, scrubbing him all over as if he were a shirtling. A hasty drying, and then he was bade dress in his father's oldest horsefolk clothes. Wool britches with a band of decorative weaving midway down, tied below the knee to shorten them for his shorter legs, a faded wool shirt that came to his knees with more bands of color on the sleeves, a horsehair-rope belt, thick wool socks.

His grandfather led their two horses—ponies, the townsfolk called them—to the door, just visible in the light from the lamp inside. No saddles, but wool-stuffed pads held on with a girth and a sheepskin over all. His grandfather accepted the pack his mother handed him, and threw himself up onto the lead horse's back.

Oktar had seen that before but never accomplished it. Town boys who rode used saddles with stirrups, and climbed on boxes to mount. His father picked him up and set him on the horse. "Don't fall off," he said. "And learn better."

"But shoes—" Oktar said, fumbling in the dark for reins. He couldn't find them.

"Horsefolk don't walk," his grandfather said from ahead of him. "They ride." He clucked to the horses and they moved off down the dark street. Oktar's belly writhed inside, but he had already spewed everything he had; he clung to the sheepskin and wondered if he would survive the day.

As light revealed the land around them, Oktar knew they were north of the town, riding north, winterwards as the horse-folk said, and the reason he hadn't been able to feel the rein was that he had none—his grandfather held Oktar's horse's rein as well as his own in his one good hand. The horses moved at a brisk walk, ears forward, alongside a stone wall with sheep on the other side of it. Oktar turned to look behind. Nothing of the town showed but a blur of smoke in the distance.

Eventually, the stone wall turned away around the bulge of a hill, and nothing was in front of them but rolling land, grass with stones showing here and there, and clumps of trees in the hollows. Oktar no longer felt nauseated, but he was hungry and thirsty and all of yesterday's bruises and scrapes hurt. So did his legs. Ahead of him, his grandfather's back was straight, shoulders level, legs dangling easily.

That posture signaled, as clearly as words, that the old man did not want to hear anything from his grandson. Not complaints, not questions, not chatter. As day brightened around them, Oktar heard a new noise—a droning sound that he finally recognized as his grandfather…singing. Singing in the horsefolk tongue, of course. Oktar did not understand the words, and whatever it was had no melody like the songs the townsfolk sang in the taverns or while working at their crafts. What it did have was rhythm, the rhythm of the horses, of their hooves and the sway of their bodies, the swish of their tails. Oktar found himself humming in the same tuneless way, minus words.

They rode on through the morning as the ground rose and lowered but mostly rose. They passed through a wood where birds racketed away from them on noisy wings and out again onto a stony slope tufted with patches of reed. Oktar saw many trails beaten into the earth by unknown feet...some narrower, some wider. Sheep? Horses? Wild animals? He had no idea. He had never been so far from town; he had never meant to be where he was, and it confused him. So much sky overhead, so wide a land, so empty of people.

When the sun was high overhead and they were riding alongside a narrow, fast-moving stream, his grandfather stopped; Oktar's horse stopped too, lowered its head, and blew a long, rattling sigh. Now his grandfather turned to him.

"Ah. You did not fall off. That is good. We rest horses, water horses, let them feed."

"We get off?" Oktar asked. He wanted to ease his legs, lie down on the grass and rest.

"No! We are horsefolk: we ride. Watch and learn, foal." His grandfather nudged his horse into the water; Oktar's followed, lowered its head to drink. His grandfather tossed Oktar's rein back to him without warning; Oktar reached but didn't catch it, and almost fell off. The horse ignored the rein trailing in the water. "Dig your toes in girth...lean forward, bracing on neck... pull up on mane behind ears."

Oktar managed this on the third try, clutching his mount's neck, and the horse's head came up from the water.

"Now take rein," his grandfather said.

Oktar let go the neck with one arm and reached. His horse swung sideways, away from his weight. He fell into the cold water with a splash.

"Stupid," his grandfather said. "Since already wet, fill water-flasks."

Oktar clambered up, fighting the pull of the knee-deep water, his wet wool clothes heavy with it, his feet flinching from the sharp edges of rock. His grandfather threw the flasks, again without warning; this time he caught one, but the other splashed in the water and immediately bobbed away.

"GET IT!" his grandfather said. Oktar stumbled and slipped downstream; his socks were no real protection from the rocks. Finally, the flask caught between two rocks and he grabbed it before it slipped away, then splashed back to where his grandfather sat on his mount. "Fill."

He started to dip the flasks in the water, but his grandfather growled. He stopped.

"Up there." His grandfather jerked his head to indicate upstream. "Clean water. Not near horses."

When he had the flasks full, Oktar splashed back to hand them up. His feet were bruised by rocks, aching from cold. His grandfather looked down at him. "Drink one swallow. Then give flask. Catch your horse."

His horse. He looked around wildly. His horse had crossed the stream and now grazed on the far side, the rein trailing.

"And take off socks before you walk on the land. Wring dry, tuck in shirt."

The socks were not dry but cold and damp when he dropped them down the neck of his shirt. Carefully, wincing at the rocks under his feet, he made it to the other side of the creek and up onto the muddy bank. The horse eyed him and ambled on a few steps. At least the ground, once he was up, had grass on it. He walked toward the horse; the horse moved away. No matter how he tried, he could not get within reach of that trailing rein.

"Sit down, fool! And call horse."

He sat down: his legs were shaky anyway. But call the horse? How?

"I taught you horse-calling chant; were you not listening?"

That droning song? Oktar hadn't understood any of the words, but the rhythm stuck with him. He tried it without words. His grandfather joined in, this time facing him; he tried to copy all the sounds. From behind him he heard a slight swish, then a warm breath caressed the back of his neck. Finally, the horse bumped him with its muzzle. Cautiously, he reached back with one hand and felt the rein in the grass and grasped it.

"Now you turn, sitting, and breathe into horse nose."

That was ridiculous. But he had no choice; he wiggled around and faced the horse, whose muzzle was then only a handspan from his face. From there on the ground, the horse looked impossibly tall. The horse reached out to sniff, and Oktar breathed carefully into one of the large nostrils, then the other. The horse blew slobber all over his face. Oktar wiped it off on his sleeve, then reached out to scratch under the horse's chin, something he remembered his father doing.

"Now up, one down jerk on rein, put leg over neck, pull mane up, horse lift you."

Oktar followed these directions with misgiving, and the horse's abrupt lift almost made him fall again. He squirmed back to a balanced position, but behind him was the bulge of the pad and sheepskin. He had no idea how he was going to get back onto it. His grandfather offered no advice. Oktar tried one thing after another, finally discovering that bracing his knees on the horse's shoulder blades and his arms on the neck allowed him to raise his backside enough to lift himself back into the hollow his morning's ride had created.

"Follow me this way," his grandfather said, and rode out of the creek on the far side.

Oktar's horse followed. He sat on the sheepskin, his rump warming up a little but the rest of him shivering in the wind that blew from the north down the little valley they followed. His damp socks, a cold lump next to his belly, warmed very slowly as he rode. He clutched the single rein tightly, not sure what to do with it—he had never seen a horse ridden with a single rein.

His grandfather sang. Oktar's horse walked a little faster until it was almost beside his grandfather's horse. His grandfather did not look at him. Sometime in the afternoon, when his clothes had dried, his grandfather handed him one of the flasks.

"One swallow. Don't drop it."

The flask had a thong loop through the neck. After taking a swallow, Oktar worked the end of the loop through his belt and around the belly of the flask so it hung at his side, as his grandfather's hung. They rode on. Oktar's stomach ached, demanding food. He had no food. He wasn't sure his grandfather had food. When the sun had dropped well behind one of the hills, his grandfather stopped his horse and rolled lightly off its back. He handed his rein to Oktar.

"Hold this. Wait." He took a long time untying the pack, lifting it one-armed from the horse, opening it on the ground. Most of the bulk was a pair of wool cloaks; inside them were four small packets. Then his grandfather looked at him. "Get down. Do this." He took the rein of his horse back from Oktar and tucked it into his belt.

Oktar slid off awkwardly, biting his lip when his bruised feet hit the ground. He tucked his rein as his grandfather had. His grandfather was doing something with the girth of his own horse's pad. Oktar looked…there was a knot, sort of. He found it on his horse, worked it loose, then pulled off the pad and sheepskin.

"Take off this." His grandfather was pulling the bridle off his horse; Oktar did the same, wondering how they would keep the horses from wandering away. But the two horses walked into the creek, drank, then set to grazing along the creek's edge.

Supper was a handful of raw oats—one for him, one for his horse, who lipped it from his hand and then walked off to graze again. He had never eaten raw oats; he had thought them food for horses. But he was hungry, so he chewed and swallowed without complaint. His grandfather brought back some leaves of a plant Oktar didn't recognize and gave him two. He ate the bitter leaves, drank the four swallows of water his grandfather ordered.

Oktar had never slept anywhere but on a straw-stuffed bag on the floor of his father's house, where walls kept out the wind and rain. Now, for the first time, he lay on the ground under stars, wrapped in one of the cloaks, the hill wind finding every opening and every damp fiber of his clothes. His grandfather had shown him how to fold the pad to support his head and use the sheepskin under his neck and upper body.

"Demons in ground steal heart," his grandfather said. "Never lie down on ground without sheepskin."

In the morning, he rolled the pack up with his grandfather's instructions, put the pad and sheepskin back on his horse, then—this time without difficulty—got his horse to lift him up again. His grandfather made him get off. "Girth loose," he said. Oktar tightened it until the old man nodded. The horse sighed heavily but lifted Oktar up on its neck again. He squirmed back into place, wishing he wasn't as sore.

"We go faster or no food," his grandfather said. "Lean back." And booted his mount into a bouncy trot.

Oktar's horse followed, and Oktar grabbed for mane. Leaning back made no sense, but he did it and then took the pounding on his tailbone until his grandfather said "Hyah!" to his horse and both of them broke into a faster gait. Smoother, too, a sort of up-and-down rocking motion.

The land came at them faster. Soon, the creek was narrow enough to step over and then just a trickle in the grass, and the horses were lunging up a steeper slope.

"Hoy!" his grandfather said when they were high enough Oktar could see over the top; the horses slowed to a halt. On the far side of the rise, the land was a tumbled mass of hills, with a distant line of higher ground against the sky.

"We go down a little. Never stop on ridge." His grandfather's horse picked its way down slowly; Oktar followed. His grandfather's horse stopped, lowered its head. "You never drop rein," Oktar's grandfather said. "But you stand on horse back."

To Oktar's surprise, the old man bent over, put his crooked hand on his horse's withers, got his knees on his horse's back, and then stood up, still holding the rein in his good hand. He looked completely at ease. "You!" he said to Oktar.

Oktar used both hands on his mount's withers and slowly—breathing hard—got his knees up. It felt far worse than sitting, sore as his rump was. He felt unbalanced and he wasn't even on his feet.

"Look at hill, not grass!" Oktar obeyed. "Tuck feet under—stand!"

Wobbling, nearly but not quite falling, Oktar finally made it to his feet, arms wide, the rein still clutched in his sweaty heart-hand. He swayed, but caught himself…and then began to feel stable.

"Now we go," his grandfather said, pulling on his horse's rein.

Up came the head. His grandfather said something in horsefolk talk, and his horse walked off, while he stood on its back as if rooted to it.

Oktar's horse lifted its head—the movement of muscles in its back almost threw him—and walked after the other. Oktar half-crouched, trying to stay in balance with it, but they were going downslope, the horse picking its way with uneven steps over small rocks and around larger ones. Oktar's toes clung to the sheepskin, digging into the fleece...and there ahead was his grandfather, straight as a pole. He could see, from behind, how his grandfather's knees were slightly bent, and his hips moved with the horse's movement, while his shoulders stayed level. Oktar tried to copy that, but his legs were shaking with the effort by the time his grandfather turned to look at him.

"Now down," his grandfather said, with a nod that might have been approval or not. He sat down on his mount and did not wait to see if Oktar had made it back to the horse's back before kicking his own into the faster rocking gait.

Oktar grabbed mane and managed to stay on, just barely. He reeled in the length of rein he'd let out. He was shaky, hungry, but...he had stood up on the back of a horse, a moving horse. He'd never done that before. None of the boys he'd fought had done that. He imagined showing them...but his grandfather's horse jumped something ahead of him. He felt his horse gather itself, a great shove—a jolting landing—and he was off-balance, losing his grip on the mane—he was falling. He hit the ground hard, rolled over rocks, and finally lay still, stunned. His shoulder hurt, his back hurt. He tried to sit up and his head spun. He heard hoofbeats coming toward him.

"Is not my blood! Must be false."

Oktar looked. His grandfather was sitting on his horse,

looking up at the sky. His own horse was standing a distance away, the rein dragging and the sheepskin pulled awry.

"Cannot be. My seed does not fall off horse. Twice in two days." The old man spat aside. "Not my son's son.

Something rumbled. Oktar stared. The morning's milky blue sky now curdled into clouds, thickened more, darkened at the base, and a roiling tower of white rose high, gleaming in the sun.

"I try. I tell him. Has no…nothing of horse in him."

A louder rumble, then a roar; Oktar's ears popped. A cold wind buffeted him; the horses turned tail to it, heads down. He struggled to his feet, only to be battered by a fall of rocks—of ice, he realized, hard cold lumps falling out of the cloud that now broke right on top of him. He fell to the ground, covering his head with his arms, as the ice pounded his back, his legs, his arms. What about his grandfather? He tried to look; through the confusing blur of falling ice, he saw his grandfather's horse…and on the ground, a dark lump. His grandfather was down? Hurt?

Despite the battering ice, Oktar forced himself up, staggering, slipping on the ice that now covered the ground, ice-rocks battering his head, to get to his grandfather. His grandfather lay still, his pack over his head.

"Granfer! Are you—" At the sound of his voice, his grandfather peered out from under the pack.

"You! Why come?"

"I thought you were hurt."

"Use eyes. Under horse no ice falls. Put head under."

Oktar put his head under the horse's belly, above his grandfather. Nothing hit his head. A last few lumps of ice pounded his back and legs, and then it was rain, hard and cold. He shivered; he couldn't help it. Then his teeth chattered. His grandfather blew a long, horselike sound through his lips.

"Get under all the way, stupid one."

When the storm passed, they rode on, over the melting lumps of ice and the wet grass. Oktar's sheepskin, sodden with rain, hung over his horse's rump; he walked, leading his mount, his bare feet so cold from the ice, he could not feel the bruises. His grandfather rode ahead, not speaking to him but muttering continually to the horses, who bobbed their heads as if they understood.

Home was too far behind to imagine, that cold night.

Two days later, they topped a rise to see far ahead a herd of animals grazing on the plain. His grandfather stood up on his horse, shading his eyes.

"See pole? See colors?"

Oktar had no idea where to look but, in trying to follow his grandfather's gaze, saw a flash of color that was not grass or rock: red. Fluttering.

"Is ours," his grandfather said. He threw back his head and let out a long, wavering cry, then another, then barked like a dog four times.

"What is—"

"Quiet. Wait."

Oktar looked around, seeing nothing but grass blowing in the wind, hearing nothing but wind hissing in the grass. The herd was mere dark specks against the tawny grass, moving slowly away from them.

Then—between one turn of his head and the next—someone appeared, not four horse-lengths away. Man and horse, the man sitting as Oktar's grandfather sat, as if his backbone grew from the horse's back. The same dark hair, but unstreaked by any gray, hung in braids adorned with beads and feathers. A horse-folk face, wide, the color the townsfolk called saddle leather, high cheekbones under ruddy cheeks, black eyes like his grandfather's and his own. The same clothes, with the same pattern woven into the pants and shirt sleeves, the long shirt belted, the vest over it open in front, showing a red lining. On his head a twisted scarf, red and yellow, with one end hanging down behind. And on this man's feet, knee-high boots whose soles were embroidered in brilliant colors, set with chips of bone or shell. The man had pulled his toes up, as if to make sure they saw every detail of the intricate design.

How did he walk on those, Oktar wondered. He must, but how? The colors were bright, undimmed by dirt. He glanced at his grandfather. For a long moment, his grandfather did not move or speak. Then his grandfather tipped his head up toward the sky and began chanting in the horsefolk tongue. The other man said nothing, sat motionless on his horse. His grandfather paused in the chant and gestured at Oktar, then fell silent.

The man looked at Oktar. He had the same beady black eyes as Oktar's grandfather and father, with the same tattoos in swirls and dots covering the heart-hand side of his face, and the same expression on it: contempt for the boy who didn't measure up. The man opened his mouth and said something short and emphatic. Oktar couldn't understand the words, but the tone confirmed the eyes: contempt.

His grandfather rode forward, held out his withered arm, and shouted, as loud as Oktar had ever heard him, right in the man's face; the man's horse pinned its ears and pivoted away. The man jerked the rein, brought it back around. The two men stared at each other a long moment, silent.

Then the man uttered another phrase, in a completely different tone, turned his horse, and the horse picked up a brisk trot.

"Come!" Oktar's grandfather followed the man without a

backward look, only that one word, and Oktar rode after him, his stomach clenching.

These were "his people"? This man, of the same tribe as his grandfather and father, this man who disliked him on sight, as the horsefolk back in town had, as *everyone* had? Would he ever find anyone who would give him a chance?

For the first time since leaving home, the hateful voices in his head drowned out everything around him. The boys at the grange, the horsefolk adults, the Marshal, the market judicar, everyone he had ever known: they all hated him; they always had.

He glared at his grandfather's receding back, at the other man. He hated them—the way they sat their horses, the way they looked at him, the way they rode on, paying no attention to him, despising him.

He yanked at the rein; his horse threw its head up but stopped. The distance between him and his grandfather length-ened. Fine. Let him go on. Let him go back to the tribe; they were not Oktar's people. Not now, not ever.

He pulled his horse's head around and booted it in the ribs; it turned a tight circle, shaking its head. It wanted to follow the others. But he did not. He would go back—not to the same house, to his father's anger and his mother's scoldings and the town that hated him. He would find another town. There must be one somewhere.

He tried again to turn his horse, this time using the few words he now knew, and the horse wiggled its ears and took a few hesitant steps before trying to swing around again. He said the words again, louder, kicked with both legs, and the horse moved on the direction he meant. He sat back against the trot, kicked again, and it picked up a canter. Behind him, he heard a yell, the sound of hooves. He kicked, kicked with each stride, until the horse was galloping, then leaned forward. He had no thought left but escape, no thought of the days traveled, the food he did not have, anything but away, escape, freedom.

Then his horse skidded to a sudden halt, Oktar's fingers and legs lost their grip, and he slid off the horse's back, right over its lowered neck, onto the ground. Again. He wanted to sink into that ground before his grandfather arrived, before another humiliation. The ground did not cooperate. He blinked, opened his eyes, and saw in front of him two dark hooves, and between them a dark muzzle. His horse? He looked up, into the face of a horse he had never seen, a peculiar yellowish color, with a long dark forelock, and two astonishing dark eyes looking into his.

Whuff! Its breath smelled of the grass and herbs under his face. The nostrils quivered, coming nearer. Without thinking, he breathed back into them, lifted a hand to touch that muzzle. The horse's upper lip extended a little, touched his hand, then the horse sniffed up his arm, finger to wrist to elbow to shoulder... and, the next thing, he knew had gripped his shirt in its teeth and lifted him as if he weighed nothing, setting him on his feet. Then it let go and stepped back.

Nearby, his horse stood, watching not him but the other horse. The new one, he could see now, had a body all that golden yellow color with legs dark to the knees and hocks, a dark mane and tail, and a dark stripe down the back. And—even he could tell this—it was a mare. Every story he'd been told brought a sudden chill down his backbone, weakness to his legs. This was a dun horse—a dun *mare*—a daughter of the Mare of Plenty, a mare among mares, the herd's wise leader.

The mare cocked her head, then reached out and took his hand in her teeth. Her big square yellow teeth closed very gently around his fingers, then tugged just a little. He took a step forward. She released his hand, nodded like a human, came closer and butted him with her head. He stumbled back; she turned sideways to him, lowered her head to the ground and ripped up a mouthful of grass. One of those big dark eyes watched him; the ear on that side pointed to him. When he did not move, she gave another loud *Whuff!* and stamped the near foreleg.

He knew what she wanted. But it was impossible. If she was the Mare of Plenty, consort of the Windsteed, mother of all the herds of the horsefolk, no human dared mount her. She was not to be ridden.

The mare swung her hindquarters closer to him, and her tail lashed him. Then she presented her neck again, this time looking at him with both eyes, both ears pricked.

Get on, fool of a boy. Clear as if she had human speech.

Would she run away with him? Would she buck him off? Trample him?

Only if you stand there.

It was hard to take that step, hard to lift his leg and step over that lowered neck, hard to imagine what it would be like—and as he thought that, the mare jerked her head up and he found himself sliding right over her low withers and onto her bare back. She stood motionless a moment, then walked toward his grandfather and the other man, both of them now only a few lengths away, staring at him in a very different way.

His horse—the one he had been riding—trailed alongside, its head near the mare's flank. As the mare walked toward, and then past, his grandfather, the two men turned their horses to ride one on either side.

"You were run away."

His grandfather sounded scornful, as usual. But no familiar surge of anger came; he could scarcely recall what he'd been doing or why. Under him, the mare's back swayed, and from her emanated a sense of comfort and safety he had not felt since early childhood, since the days his mother had carried him, had protected him from the older children, before he knew that who he was, who she was, who they all were, made any difference.

"What means you?" his grandfather asked.

He had no words to answer he thought his grandfather would understand. "She came to me," he said.

The other man laughed, and said something to his grandfather that made his grandfather laugh.

"She knows horse from ass," his grandfather said. "You are son's son after all." He reined back, moved alongside the horse Oktar had been riding, and scooped up the trailing rein in his withered arm, grabbing it then with his good hand. He moved back up beside Oktar. "You take rein. I go."

Oktar took the rein his grandfather held out; the other man said something emphatic to his grandfather. The words hissed and clicked; all three horses pricked their ears.

"It make trouble, I go there," Oktar's grandfather said to him. "I not go. He want, give me food. I stay here, but only tonight."

"You're leaving me? I can't talk—"

"You learn. You learn, son's son. You horse-folk. *She* says." He pointed his elbow at the mare; she flicked an ear.

"But I don't know—Who is he?"

"Family," his grandfather said. He waved his hand; the other man nodded, and kicked his horse forward.

The mare followed; his grandfather's horse stood still; his grandfather looked past them all at something Oktar could not see. The horse Oktar had ridden moved along without tugging on the rein, and Oktar, twisting to look back, saw his grandfather sitting perfectly straight, his withered arm invisible from this angle.

Fear shook him. What was he supposed to do? He had not imagined his grandfather leaving him alone with these people, these strangers whose language he could not speak, in a place where he knew nothing. Under him, the mare's calm, steady presence went on, her walk swinging her belly from side to side, forcing his legs and seat to adjust. There was nothing to fear, that walk said, speaking to his legs and his rump and his back. *Relax. Move with me.* He breathed more easily, relaxed a little.

The man riding on his knife-side said nothing to him, and they rode, and rode, and behind him his grandfather dwindled in size as if literally shrinking, and then they rode down a steeper slope and he could not see his grandfather at all. Fear clutched him again; he gasped, stiffened, reached for the mare's rein—and there was no rein, he was sitting on her bare back, without any way to control her. Again her steady gait, the sense of safety imposed by her unhurried but purposeful stride, eased the fear. While he was on her back, nothing could hurt him, and she would not let him fall. He was able to breathe, to look ahead, where the herd was now visibly closer. He did not understand it. He did not understand anything.

As they came nearer, the man beside him turned heartward, to circle the herd. Now Oktar could see other riders, and beyond them, on a low rise, dun-colored lumps. Houses? He had no idea what they were, but the mare and the man's horse both picked up the pace a little. He could see other riders, too. As they neared the houses, he realized they were round, and not houses at all. He had no word for them. Children ran between them, calling out in high voices, then stopped and stared when the man who still rode beside him raised a hand. Women pushed aside curtains from openings and came out to stare as well. Beyond these…things, he could see other riders approaching.

In the center of the inner ring of the round rooms, the dun mare stopped. The man looked at Oktar, said something Oktar did not understand, then sighed. He called out, and one of the women came to him, holding out a pair of worn boots. Still on his horse, the man took off one boot at a time, put on the boots the woman handed him, and she took the boots he had worn. He swung off his horse. The dun mare shivered, all the skin of her back telling Oktar to get off. He did so, wincing at the pain as his feet hit the ground, smooth-packed dirt though it was. The mare blew warm on his arm: reassurance.

The man said nothing more; Oktar looked around. Older men and women sat on piles of pillows next to openings in the round houses. They all stared at him. So did those now coming into the central circle, those walking from round rooms farther away, surrounded by children, and those who had been riding, some of them older children. They murmured to one another in their speech, but no one spoke to him, or loudly.

Oktar, surrounded by what his grandfather had called *our* people, recognized his father, mother, and grandfather in those faces. All, like his own, roundish rather than long. All, like his own, the same shade of yellow-brown, the same black eyes, the same black hair. The man who had met them began to talk, addressing the group, talking fast. Oktar felt the dun mare behind him breathing on his spine. Warm…warm…warm. He put a hand behind his back; the mare mumbled along it with her lips, then blew slobber into his palm. He wiped his hand on the seat of his britches.

The mare hung her head over his shoulder just as an older man, braids going gray, rose from his stack of pillows. He wore a crescent shape wrapped in scarlet thread hanging from a thong around his neck, and rings of plaited horsehair on both thumbs—one black, one white. He pointed at Oktar and said "Nyesh! Evahk!" The crowd shifted a little but said nothing.

The mare leaned into Oktar's shoulder, her head thrust out in front of him, and whinnied; he felt the sound in his own body, not just in his ears.

An old woman stood up, all her hair gone gray. She also wore a crescent, hers bound in brilliant blue, and a crown of plaited horsehair on her head: red, black, golden, and white. She pointed at Oktar, then the man who had spoken. "Issnah. Vahktahn."

The mare stamped a forefoot and pushed Oktar forward, closer to both of them. Oktar knew they must be important but had no idea who they were. The man must be a ruler, but the old woman? Was she his wife? Mother? Sister? And what were they saying?

The old woman chirped; the mare kept pushing Oktar forward, nudging his back with her chest, until the mare could reach the old woman's hand, held out flat with a brown lump of something on it. The mare lipped it up then nodded up and down three times. The old woman bowed, hands together. Then she turned to the man. "Issnah. Selehalyanya."

He sighed, mouth pinched together, then nodded. "Selehalyanya."

Everyone said it then. Oktar wondered what it meant; he knew *Alyanya* but could they mean the Lady of Peace? He said the word himself, softly, doubting his hearing of it. The mare lifted her head high, whinnied once more, then turned away from him, turning back. Oktar turned, saw the people make a lane for the mare, who trotted away, ears pricked forward.

The mare was like his grandfather. Going away. Leaving him. He wanted to cry; he wanted to run after her, but the old woman now had his wrist in her hand, shaking it for his attention.

"You—sire-sire brave man. You look him much. You learn talk, you learn horse, you grow man."

Oktar nodded. He had no choice. He could not run away there; he knew no place to go.

"You name?"

"Oktar."

"Oktar." She nodded. "You come—I take you."

Her hand on his wrist was bony, the skin sun-darkened. He waited for her to move; he would follow, he knew. But she stood there, gazing around at the people. She pointed and called out. A boy a half head taller than Oktar and a girl his own height came toward them. The boy said something, low and fast. The old woman shook her head.

"The Mare chose. You teach." She looked at Oktar. "Dargan—Sekklan. Not too old teach. You, not too young learn. The Mare chose."

The End

Author's Note on Dream's Quarry

Sekkin's trial of adulthood takes place in the vast grassland lying north of Fintha, Tsaia, and Lyonya, the age-old range of horse nomads. When a child acquires their second permanent molar in both jaws, they are sent out alone with three horses, not to return until they have killed an enemy of the clan. The preparation for this task includes an attempt to achieve a vision through fasting and other trials. Those who do have a prophetic dream gain extra status if they perform the exact feat of courage in the dream—and claimed it before leaving.

Publication note: "Dream's Quarry" was initially published in *Horse Fantastic*, DAW, ed. Martin H. Greenberg & Rosalind M. Greenberg, 1991.

DREAM'S QUARRY

Today she was a woman. She had eaten her last child meal the day before; today they had feasted her with blood and ironmeal and stonedust for strength and endurance, with stolen southern wine for courage. Sitting crosslegged on the fine diamond-patterned carpet, Sekkin wore the new clothes that proclaimed her status. Knee-high boots, embroidered all over the soles with expensive scarlet thread and tiny chips of iridescent shell from river clams, replaced the low rawhide boots of a child. She would not touch ground to walk while she wore them, lest the embroidery break. Her outer tunic and matching pants were of softest leather, supple as cloth, instead of coarse wool. On the carpet before her were her clan's gifts: an unnamed sword, a short bow backed with sinew, a light lance with a point of dwarf-wrought steel, a drinking horn on its thong, a leather bag for food. They had painted her face with luck charms: Stormwind Clan's spirals and Guthlac's horns and the hoofprints of the Windsteed and the Mare of Plenty. They had sung over her, dancing around her carpet throne until the dust turned the sun orange. Now she waited, while her father and uncles brought her horses, horses she had never mounted, horses they'd traded for this purpose from another clan. And the clan wizard knelt before her, asking of her dreams.

Everyone waited for her answer. "Will you name the blood you bring?" she was asked, three times in the ritual, with the hoof-chimes ringing after each. And then, when she did not answer, the final question: "Will you seek a dream's quarry?"

"I will," she said, eyes focused somewhere beyond the crowd. She felt the answer as they did, a cold tremor inside. A wavering cry, then silence, fell across them.

"You followed a true dream?" asked the wizard.

"I did—I followed a dun mare's hoofprints, and the hoof-prints filled with water." That was a great omen, as she knew. No one spoke; even the horses were silent.

"Will you name the blood?" asked the wizard. It was her last chance. She could refuse, but if she named she would have to do that, exactly that, whatever it was, or be exiled forever. It was a way to test the truth of dreams, or of dreamers.

But those who named the blood, and fulfilled their claim, won honor in the clan, great honor. She waited, remembering her dream, and savoring their attention, then dipped her head slightly. "I will name the blood," she said. "I will ride with Guthlac, and claim a Huntsman of that Hunt."

At that the wizard fell back, and touched his charms: brow, throat, and wrist. She watched through slitted eyes the crowd's response. Fear, first, for themselves, and then astonishment and even anger. She was daring much; she risked more than herself, to challenge Guthlac's Huntsmen. Her failure could bring the Hunt down on Stormwind Clan itself. But the Horsebreeder had stood, sealing the ceremony: as the mare flirts, so the breeding goes. She had the right to make that choice, and the duty to abide by it.

"So it shall be for Sekkin," said the wizard loudly. "She shall not walk the earth, her foot shall not touch the ground, until she brings the blood of Guthlac's Huntsman to Stormwind's tents. By the luck of the Windsteed's foals, by hoof and mane, may this woman prove herself Clan-kin of Stormwind."

The crowd's murmur was low and busy; through it she heard the hoofbeats of the horses her male kin brought. She did not turn to see; custom forbade such curiosity. A Stormwind child who could not mount and ride any horse, known or unknown, deserved no chance at adulthood. The sound of the stride told her much. Two were nomad-bred, and perfectly sound: the same quick four-beat gait she had heard all her life. One had a longer stride, a lighter cadence, like dancing; she imagined a slender racer from far away.

They stopped behind her. A leadrope dropped into her hand; her father's hand opened for her if she chose. She tucked the leadrope into her belt, and gathered her gifts without moving from her seat. Bow over the shoulder, sword through the other side of the belt, lance to brace her turn. Drinking horn tucked into her tunic, along with the empty foodsack. Now she looked. She sat beneath the front hooves of a dun mare, best of omens; on the saddle she could see a quiver of arrows, a rolled storm cloak. Behind was a bay, with a second saddle and a roll of blanket. Behind that was a black, a tall black horse of the southlands, Finthan perhaps or even Tsaian, unsaddled but bearing a long coil of rope around the neck as well as a halter.

She ignored her father's hand, and rolled to her knees. She had seen nothing amiss, but she must check the girth herself. It was tight; her father had not tricked her. She reached up and slid the lance into the loops on the saddle, then checked the bridle carefully. Ready.

She could mount in several ways. Her boots might withstand a single step, though for every broken strand of thread her bride-price would fall. Or she could use her father's hand, and half-vault upward from her knees to the saddle. Or she could hope the dun mare had been trained to lift a rider from the ground—most Stormwind mounts were so trained. But if she tried that and failed—if the mare spooked, and dumped her on the ground, that would end her trial of adulthood before it began.

Slowly, resisting the pressure of the crowd's curiosity, she scratched the mare under the chin, gently coaxing her head down. The mare did not resist. On her knees, Sekkin edged nearer, into position. No one spoke. With a last brief prayer to the Windsteed, and a touch of the piece of hoof on its thong around her neck, Sekkin threw herself up and sideways, flinging her leg over the mare's lowered neck. The mare jerked her head up; Sekkin clung, off-balance an instant, but did not fall. She slid back to the saddle, then, and settled herself, enjoying the dry, tongue-clicking applause of the clan.

"Ride with the Windsteed, Sekkin," her father shouted. "Hunt the distance and find blood." The crowd broke into a chant, her name and the clan's together, good luck, good hunting. The dun mare shied, but Sekkin caught her with legs and hands, turned her away, and booted her into a quick jog away from camp. The bay lined out smoothly behind them, and the black swung wide, snorting, to the right of the bay.

Already it was past noon, and as warm as it would be so early in spring. Sekkin jogged on, heading winterwards, for the next water lay some hours' ride away, and she did not want to sleep dry. As she rode, she checked her equipment, shifting the sword to its own saddle loops, and tying the bow to a knot of mane with the Stormwind secret knot. At least, she thought, it was her own saddle, the saddle she had made two years before and broken in on her favorite mount. Rising high before and behind, padded with tailhair and sheep's wool, it was easy riding for the miles she must cover. Her legs swung free above the early grass. Horse-folk did not use stirrups as the lowlanders did, and Sekkin was glad of it. Stirrups marked bootsoles: only the horsefolk could prove they never walked. Despite the lack of sleep, the strange food, the stinging burns on her feet inside the padded boots—a reminder not to walk, even barefoot—she felt elated. She had challenged Guthlac—she had named a great blood—she would be the first of her father's children to seek a dream's quarry, and bring it home.

By sunfall, she was far out of sight of the clan, and even its dust cloud had sunk to a smudge on the summerward way. The dun mare had shown a smooth, distance-eating stride, and all three horses had calmed. She had found the slough she'd hoped for, a shallow wing-shaped band of water, fresh enough for her and the horses. As they drank, she lowered her drinking horn on its cord, emptied it, and refilled it. She rode slowly along the margin, letting the horses crop tender grass almost at will, while she emptied that horn slowly. Then she halted them, and reeled in the other two horses. Leaning over, she checked the girth of the bay's saddle, and tightened it. She transferred her weapons to the bay, and the blankets from that saddle to the dun, trusting the mare now not to shy or jerk away. Finally, she vaulted to the bay, and took up the reins. When she was satisfied that all was well, she unbridled the dun, looping the bridle around her neck, and fastened her leadrope to the bay's saddle, tying the black's lead to her. Then she rode back to the water, and refilled her drinking horn a final time.

Now she must decide where to spend the night. The horses might graze here peacefully, but so any wandering wolf pack might come. In the last light she rode splashing through the water, noting the black horse's high-stepping reluctance. Then she aimed the bay's nose winterwards, and let herself sink into the light doze of her training.

She passed several days that way, riding always winterwards as the Clan reckoned it, into the face of winter's wind, with the summer wind at her back. She ate lightly, of what she could hunt from horseback, or berries from the rare clumps of bushes around some spring. And she talked to the three horses, the foundation of her future herd when she came home in triumph, naming them with names no one else would know. Now they all came to her, eager for her gentle hands on head and body, responsive to her and to each other.

This was the way all the Clans had started, by the songs they sang: a woman with three horses, riding alone in the empty lands, had called the Windsteed in a dream, and the Windsteed had brought foals to her mares. Then a wicked man tricked the Windsteed into bondage, but the woman killed the man and freed the Windsteed, and she herself bore a child as a gift of the Mare of Plenty...so it was sung. Alone on the grasslands, with the wind and her horses, Sekkin felt happy, whole of soul and body, as she never had before. She had no need to walk herself, with twelve black hooves to serve her. As for those functions the southern folk preferred to do in private, on the ground, a single nomad in an empty land could perform quite well on horseback. She had done so from childhood.

But on a day it occurred to her that although she was happy, she was no nearer her dream, and the blood she must bring. Guthlac's wild Hunt rode the winter wind, and she had gone winterwards now so far that a blue haze grew along the line of the setting sun. She had heard of mountains to the far sunsetting and winterwards, but had never seen them. But where was Guthlac?

Where was the Huntsman? Had the summerwind driven them away, and must she wander until winter?

That day she rode upright, looking winterwards as hard as she could, hoping for some sign that Guthlac's hunt lay not too far away. And that night, when Torre's Necklace shone above the last sunglow, she sent a prayer to Torre—for all that Torre was a southern saint, and no horsefolk deity at all. For the Horsebreeder sang that Torre's black horse was the Windsteed's foal, and not the spawn of the Black Wind of Gitres Undoer; for that, and not for her deeds, Sekkin honored her. In the dark center of the night, when the Necklace had been under the world's rim for two spans of starmoving, Sekkin first heard Guthlac's horn, far away.

It sent chills down her back but she legged the dun mare toward the sound. The Hunt would have passed; still, she might find trace of its passing. And by dawn she found trampled grass, the tracks of great horses running at full stretch, and a tangle of dark cloth in the grass that brought a frown to her.

She had heard of the blackrobe followers of Achrya, but never seen one. Among the horsefolk they were called simply blackrobes, or less commonly falkur-ste: "false-beauty", which recognized their kinship with the falkur, the beautiful, the elder singers. The dead body Sekkin found tangled in its own black robe was clearly such, the face of surpassing beauty and even in death showing the cold perilous arrogance of its kind. So this was what Guthlac Hunted—at least here, and in this time. On such a Hunt she would prefer to ride, but she was sworn to bring back Huntsman's blood, for the clan's honor and her life.

She turned the dun into that track, and rode sunrising, with day brightening in her face. Her tracker's eyes built the size of Guthlac's horses from the length of stride, the size of hoofprint, seen here and there between the thick grasses. And by midmorning, she had found another blackrobe dead, silver-sparked blood streaking the dark cloak. She kept on, switching mounts from bay to dun and back again. So far she had rested the black, but now she measured its strides against those of the Hunt, and decided to saddle the black before dark.

She came to water, a slow stream moving summerwards: the Hunt's tracks were plain in its muddy banks. One set were cloven—Guthlac himself, or his mount. She didn't know which; the stories went both ways. Her horses drank, and she refilled her drinking horn over and over, filling herself with water for the coming dry afternoon. She had seen that even the Hunt drank here, the horses spread along the bank, standing with forefeet in the water, and bootmarks as well, from some of the riders.

As the sun sank behind her, throwing her shadow ahead, she noticed how it grew taller. She had seen that before, but never thought about it. Now it seemed both ominous and hopeful: she rode toward danger and death, but became larger thereby.

Then the trail she followed disappeared, shortly before sunfall. She looked around, ahead, as best she could, standing on the saddle with a blanket over it to protect her bootsoles, and shading her eyes. No trace of the Hunt's passage lay beyond. The grass blew unmarked between her and the edges of the world. For the first time since hearing Guthlac's horn, she felt a tremor of fear. The Hunt was not mortal—or not wholly so—but as long as she had hoofprints to follow, she had felt herself at home. But for the Hunt to disappear, leap—as it seemed it must have leaped—into the air, here in the middle of the grass, that was uncanny, frightening. She stooped again to the mare's back, stretching her legs first to one side, then the other. She would wait here. Whatever happened this night, she expected no sleep.

The sun dropped under the world's rim, and her shadow melted into a soft haze of dusk. Quickly, Sekkin transferred to the bay, shifted her favorite saddle to the black. Despite her hurry, it was nearly dark when she had made her gear fast to that saddle, and arranged the leadlines as she wished. Stars pricked the dull blue sky, brightened as day faded, and merged into the patterns she knew. All she could see of the land was starlight on the grass, and the shapes of her horses, dark against it. A light movement of air stirred the grass. This time it was cold, from winterwards, smelling of ice and rock and distant forested mountains. It strengthened. She turned to face it, cupping one ear at a time out of its hum to listen for whatever might be coming.

The dun mare threw up her head. That was all the warning Sekkin got before a blackrobe sword stabbed at her, starlight flowing down the blade. She jerked the bay back; it reared, snorting. Another blackrobe had the dun, had cut the leadrope. The mare squealed and bucked, but the blackrobe held tight, and whipped her away sunrising. Sekkin tried to shift the bay near the black, dancing on the end of its lead, but the first blackrobe was still coming at her, sword moving in patterns she did not know. She had left her lance on the black's harness; with her own short sword she could not fight in front of her mount. She wheeled the bay, swung, and heard the bitter snap of her blade as the blackrobe's sword broke it like a dry stick. At that she wheeled again, kicked the bay into a flat run, and tossed the black's lead free. It would follow the bay, and her, and would run better loose.

In the dark she could see nothing of the ground; she had to trust the bay's sense. Ahead she heard the uneven hoofbeats of the dun, still fighting her rider. The black ran alongside, a bowshot off. Behind came the harsh, high call of a more blackrobes, voices as cold as their faces but less beautiful. Sekkin felt for her bow, strung it, and set an arrow to the string. The bay was catching the dun, and if she could get a shot—

Over her head the horns rang out, and the night was full of horses, before, behind, all around, racing flat out over the grass. The bay shied, nearly throwing her, as something twice its size pounded past. Sekkin's breath caught. They shone in starlight as if edged with pale flame: Guthlac's followers, the Huntsmen, the tireless. Ahead of them, visible in his own glow, Guthlac. The branching tines of his antlers caught the starlight in a silver web, his eyes glowed, his cloven hooves tossed the grass behind him as he ran. All around, above, the horns blew, music that caught her heart, bound her in the Hunt. She glanced aside, and saw other glowing eyes watching her, hands raised in salute, weapons gleaming.

But the bay had no speed for this chase. They fell back, little by little. She heard the cries as the Hunt closed on the dun mare and her burden. She kicked the bay frantically. Perhaps she could catch up with the dun, at least, but the little mare raced on, free now of the blackrobe's weight. Then one of the trailing Huntsmen turned and saw her, slowed his own mount to her speed. In the starlight his face was very fair: she almost named him falkur.

"You chose an ill mount for this," he said over the noise of the hooves.

"I had a better," Sekkin said, "But the blackrobes attacked— my sword broke—"

"Is the loose black yours?" When she nodded, he sped away, returning shortly with the black horse, running easily on its long lead. He tossed her the cut end, and she reeled the black in, letting the bay slow to a laboring canter. Then she swung over to the black, and left the bay free.

Ahead, the horns still sang, calling. She had no need to urge the black horse; it wanted nothing more than to run with that herd. She checked her gear as it ran, making sure of lance and bow, arrows and dagger. It was hard to think, with that wild music in her ears. Hard to remember what she was there for, to Hunt the Hunt itself. The black horse ran smoothly, long strides that brought the rear of the Hunt back to them. Sekkin turned to the Huntsman who had helped her, only to see a black shadow rise from the starlit grass ahead and throw itself at his horse.

The Huntsman's horse swerved, staggered, and rolled neck over croup. With a shriek the blackrobe leaped forward. Sekkin hauled her horse down, and swerved across its path, jabbing with her lance. She felt it hang in the blackrobe's cloak, thrust harder, and found herself holding a dead weight on her shaft. Before she could free it, the Hunt had turned. Two spears pierced the blackrobe besides her lance, and Guthlac strode to them. The Huntsman who had fallen lay still. She could not see if he lived.

Now the horns blared even louder. Guthlac's eyes were like wind-fired coals as he looked around at the circle of horses and riders. His voice, when he spoke, was unexpected—cool and sweet, like that of a young boy.

"Another Achryan servant—good hunting, lords and ladies." He went on. "And whose kill is this? I have not seen this lance before."

Sekkin froze. Until then she hardly realized that she had killed. She had made her first kill, the kill that made her adult, Clan-kin—or would have done so, had she not named a Huntsman as her dream's quarry. Before she could answer, that burning gaze was turned on her.

"Ah—a new member of our Company…and who may you be, Lady?"

She had to answer, dry mouth or no. "Sekkin, Lord—" she said. "Of Stormwind Clan—"

"Horsefolk," he interrupted. He was near enough now that she could see details of his face. Short tangled hair around his face, no beard of manhood, a pointed chin. Out of that tangle of hair on his head rose the twin antlers; Sekkin stared at them, fascinated. "The horsefolk," he was saying now, to the others, "have always understood hunting. Is it not so, Lady?"

She could not answer. She could not say anything, faced with Guthlac, the Hunter of Souls, in the midst of his Hunt. He took a long breath, blew it into the black horse's nostrils. The black reached out, bumped Guthlac with its nose, and rumbled a horse greeting.

"Did you choose to hunt with us, Lady of Stormwind, or were you traveling somewhere?" A mocking tone had entered his voice; it reminded her of all the tales. Sekkin sat up straighter.

"I dreamed this hunt, Lord," she said. "I followed your trail yesterday, and sought you by darkness."

A low murmur from the crowd. Guthlac turned, his cloven hooves treading a pattern she almost recognized. He reached to the blackrobe, and twitched her lance free, touched the tip to his mouth, then handed it to her. "You have sought blackrobe blood; you have chosen to hunt with me. Are you Clan-kin, Lady?"

"No, Lord. This hunt is my trial."

"This blood will free you, then, will it not?" She saw his hand reach out, silvered by starlight and darkened by blackrobe blood. And she went cold to the bone, knowing herself trapped. Hunter he might be, but Guthlac hunted more than one way; he was Lord of traps and tricks as well as the running hunt. But she had brought this on herself, and she knew she dared not lie.

"No, Lord," she said. "This blood will not free me, because I dreamed a different quarry."

"Oh—you wish to hunt longer with us, eh? Bold folk the horsebreeders have become, Lady, since my last encounter, if blackrobe blood will not suffice for Clan-kinship. What quarry did you name, then?"

"A Huntsman of Guthlac," she said, forcing herself to meet those glowing eyes. At her words they brightened from red to gold, and she heard the shocked whispers all around her. Then he laughed, the wild laugh of a careless boy.

"Bold indeed, daughter of Stormwind, and bolder to tell me so. Indeed, Lady, we have not had such a wild boast for many seasons. And which Huntsman of mine did you have in mind, Lady, and why did you seek such prey?"

Well, she would die, and leave her bones to the hunters of the air, but she would die a fighter, as she had been taught. Still meeting his eyes, she settled her lance in her grip. "Lord, I followed the ritual dream, the steps of a dun mare, and named my prey as the law requires. I saw no face, only a shape in the dark. In the dream, the Hunt rode on, laughing, and let me go."

Then they laughed, all but Guthlac, wild voices around her of many kinds. Even the horses neighed, and it seemed mockery. But Guthlac did not laugh, only looked at her coolly and turned away. Sekkin braced herself for an attack, but no one else moved; the laughter died of its own weight. Guthlac moved lightly to the fallen Huntsman and his horse, and knelt beside them. Then he called.

"Lady of Stormwind—"

"Yes, Lord."

"Come." She could not disobey that command; even had she wanted to, the black horse was already moving. It stepped carefully past the dead blackrobe, stopped at Guthlac's signal, beside the fallen horse. Somehow—she could not tell how, and did not wonder at the time—Guthlac brought a little light, silver as starlight but brighter, to that place, and she saw the fallen Huntsman. He lay twisted, partly beneath his dead mount and partly free, but his arms were slack, his hands motionless on the grass, his sword fallen away out of his grasp. She saw his chest move, and realized he was alive and yet could not live; she had seen men crushed by horses, or with broken necks, before this.

"Here is one," said Guthlac, "who cannot live. Kill him, Lady, and fulfill your vow." The light in his eyes flickered.

Sekkin stared at him. "Lord—he helped me! He caught my horse—"

"He was of my Hunt. He is dying, in pain. I give him to you, Lady, in exchange for this night's hunt. Give the deathstroke, Lady, and be free."

"But I—but he—" In her mind he had become almost a friend, the voice in the dark who caught her horse, made it possible for her to catch up with the Hunt. How could she kill a friend? Besides, would such a kill count? She had thought to kill in battle, as she killed the blackrobe, in anger or defiance, not in pity. These thoughts tangled in her mind, and Guthlac watched her with fire-red eyes, and the man at her horse's feet struggled for breath, groaning a little.

Guthlac laughed, then, mocking her confusion. "You were his death anyway, Lady—but for you he would not have been attacked. You have taken a Huntsman; be glad you have taken a blackrobe to pay for him."

And the Hunt gathered around her, closer and closer. Wildness filled the air, tightened her belly, made every breath a struggle. The black horse flattened its ears, humped its back.

"Is it a Stormwind way to kill a shadow in the dark, and

flinch from a face clearly seen? So the blackrobes kill, and all Achrya's servants. If you don't take this blood, Lady," said Guthlac, in a voice so low she could hardly hear it, "the Hunt may have a new quarry. Could you get back to your Clan, Lady, running ahead of the Hunt?" Sekkin could not control the shudder that ran down her back, as much revulsion as fear.

"But it's cruel," she said. "He helped me—"

"And does Stormwind leave lame horses to die, and injured warriors to be torn by hunters of the sky while they still breathe?" No, she knew better, but she had planned to kill her quarry fairly. Later was time enough to learn that harder lesson. All her life she had known it was done, and hated it; the only good she knew of the farmfolk gods was their claim to healing skills. "You wanted to ride with the Wild Hunt," Guthlac said, "and you wanted to take one of my Huntsmen. Lady, you had best be swift with your weapons, lest we decide you are no hunter after all, someone afraid of blood or the shades of the dead. You made your choice; abide by it."

In the silence that followed that, she heard the injured man draw a rasping breath. "Lord—" came his voice, very faint, pleading. Guthlac stamped once, shaking the ground.

"Yes!" Sekkin hardly knew what she meant by that, as her lance went down, a clean blow to the throat, and ended that torment. At once the tension eased; the other Huntsmen drew away a little. Guthlac again reached for her lance and withdrew it from the deathwound. She didn't notice when the shaft left her grasp; she was crying, her tears hot against her night-cold face. She had not believed, until then, that she herself must bear all the endings of her designs, as a mare must carry and foal what she deigns to accept from a stallion. Colt or filly, large or small, easy or hard: she was grown, and she must endure. Slower than she wanted, she regained control, gulping her sobs back. Guthlac stood before her still, holding her lance, its bloody point facing her.

"Do you fear me, Lady of Stormwind?" he asked.

Fear, sorrow, anger, and a strange peace mingled in her mind, along with the remains of that earlier excitement. She could not say it, but he nodded as if he understood, the great antlers throwing sparks of starlight at her.

"Lady, your time will come to ride with us for long and long. For now—" He touched the lance's point to her face, tracing a design on her forehead, on her cheeks. She felt a line of fire where the point touched, but she could not move. "For now, Lady, you are free of your vows, and Stormwind should count you Clan-kin. Let this be proof of the blood you shed: if any questions your scars or deeds, let that one seek answer from Guthlac." He handed back the lance, and gave a strange snort. Two nomad-bred ponies jogged up; Sekkin was not surprised to recognize her dun and bay. Guthlac breathed on both of them, and handed her their leads. "Ride summerwards, Lady: winter is mine, and I will hunt this land closely." She wheeled her horse, and the horns cried a warning note that sent all three away at a good pace. Behind her their wild laughter rose.

* * *

Sekkin returned to Stormwind Clan before Summereve, with a dun mare in foal and strange scars on her face. When she showed her bootsoles, with no thread broken or shell-chip missing, and the scars with their design of mingled hoofprints and antlers, she passed into the tent of warriors.

The End

Author's Note on Gifts

Running away from a bad situation is a common tactic of children. Usually, it doesn't work out the way the runaway hopes, though sometimes it is the only way to survive. When adults run away from responsibility, results can be worse. But a gift can be solace and inspiration. When Dall Drop-hand falls off a ledge onto a drunk one dark night, more than two lives change.

Publication note: "Gifts" was originally published in *Masters of Fantasy*, Baen Books, ed. Bill Fawcett & Brian Thomsen, 2004.

GIFTS

In the fullness of spring, with flowers everywhere and the scent of them filling the nose, Dall Drop-hand, Gory the Tall's third son, quarreled with his father and brothers, and went off to find adventure.

"You'll regret it," his father said.

"You'll come crawling back as soon as your belly gripes," said his oldest brother.

"You'll find out nobody wants a fool whose only talent is dropping things," said his second-oldest brother.

His younger brothers and two of his sisters merely jeered. But the last sister cried, and hugged him, and begged him to stay. The others watched, still laughing, and he turned away.

"Wait," she said. "I'll give you a parting gift."

"The only parting gift he needs is a kick in the pants," said his father. But he stood aside to let the girl scamper to her bed, and pull out her treasure, a bit of wood carved in the likeness of a knife. She had found it lying loose among the leaves while nutting the year before. She ran back to her brother, and put it in his hand.

"Take this," she said. "You may need it."

It was only wood, and not very sharp, but hers was the only

kind voice that day. "Are you sure, Julya?" he asked.

"I am," she said, standing straight as young children do, upright as a pine, and she flung her arms around him and kissed him. Then she stood back, and he was bound to go, a gawky lad of no particular beauty or skill, out into the world all alone, at the very season when food was shortest, for no one can live on flowers.

He walked off down the path that led to the ford, and stopped to drink deeply of that fast, cold water. He would have taken some in a waterskin, but he had no waterskin. Still it was spring, with water running fast in every brook and rill, and he was sure he would find water at need. Food was another matter. He had no bow, no line for setting snares. In all this wealth of flowers, no fruit had set but wild plums, and they were green and hard as pebbles still. His eye fell on a ruffle of green leaves trembling in the moving water. They looked very much like the greens his mother grew in the back garden. He picked off a piece, and tasted it. Yes. The very same. He picked a handful, and stuffed them into his shirt and set off away from the stream, on a path that narrowed here to a foot's width from little travel.

By midafternoon, he had passed through the woods near the stream and come out into open country, fields grown up into tall grass and flowers that reached his waist. He had lost the path in that tall growth, and found it again by stumbling over its groove; now he walked slowly, letting his feet feel their way and hoping no snake lurked below, where he could not see through the lacework of white and yellow. In the distance, the land rose in billows to blue hills, but he could not tell how far off they were.

At sunfall, he was still in the fields, wading slowly through the flowers. He trampled out a circle his own length, with the groove of the footpath running across it, and sat down. The footpath made a little tunnel, forward and back, under the tall growth. If he'd been a small animal, he could have used it as a private road and traveled hidden. The thought amused him; he wondered what it would be like to be so small, to see the meadow as a forest. For him, the footpath would make a comfortable hole for his hip, when he lay down to sleep.

The leaves he'd gathered were a limp, unappetizing mess when he pulled them from his shirt, but he ate them anyway and tried not to think of his family at their supper. He lay down then, and sat up quickly as his sister's gift poked him in the side. He pulled it out and rubbed his finger along the rib of wood. There was still enough light to see that it gleamed a little, where his sister had rubbed it with fat, but not enough to see the design that his finger felt, something carved, not deeply, into it. He kissed the thing, blessing the sister who had given it—useless though it was, it had been her treasure—and lay down to sleep with it in his hand.

He woke in darkness, uneasy, at first not knowing where he was. His shirt had rucked up, baring his back to the chill spring breezes; he yanked it down one-handed but could not go back to sleep. Around him, over him, the grass and flower-stalks rustled in the breeze. So did something else; he sat up, eyes wide. Was that more than star-shadow, that dark movement on the trail? Meadow mice, probably, or the slightly larger field rats. A stoat? A fox?

Laughter ringed him in so suddenly that he felt a shock like cold water. They were all around him, tattered shadows in the starlight, holding weapons that already pricked his back, his sides. Weapons that glinted slightly in that faint light. Laughter stilled to uneasy silence.

"Mortal man, you trespass." That voice was high, higher than his youngest sister's, but very clear.

"I'm not a man," he said. His voice broke on the absurdity of that; he had told his father he was man enough, when his father called him boy once too often.

"Not a man?" the voice asked, mocking. Laughter rimmed the circle again, and again died. "And what, pray, art thou if not man? Art too tall for rockfolk, too uncomely for elvenkind, and having speech canst not be a mere beast, despite the smell..." More laughter.

He found his voice again. "I'm a boy." Most of the elder folk were kinder to children than adults; he would claim that protection if he could. Surely if his father considered him a mere boy, so also would beings far older than his father.

"I think not," the voice said. "I think thou art man grown, at least in some things..." The voice insinuated what things, and he felt himself going hot. "And since we found thee asleep athwart our high road, man-grown as thou art, I say again: mortal man, you trespass. And for your trespass, mortal man, you shall be punished."

The shift of tone, from common to formal and back again, jerked at his mind, confused him. He fell back on childhood's excuse. "I didn't know..."

"Did not know what? That this was our highway, or that it was forbidden to such as you?"

"Either—both. I was only trying to get away from home..." That sounded lame as a three-legged cow in the night, with sharp points pricking him.

"You drew a circle across our highway," the voice said. "You drew a circle and then lay athwart, your loins on the path, and you thought nothing of it? No loss to the world then, such an oaf as you."

"But a circle is holy," he said. "A circle protects..."

Hisses all around him, as sharp as sleet on stubble; his belly went cold.

"A circle with a line across it negates the protection of the circle," the voice said. "And when that line is our highway—you have made a grave error, mortal man, and you will indeed be punished. Away from home, you wanted to go? Away from home you shall go indeed, never to return..."

His fists clenched, in his fear, and in the heart-hand his sister's gift bit into the insides of his fingers. But what use a little wooden knife-shape against the creatures here, whose sharp weapons were surely harder and sharper than wood?

He had to try. He shifted the knife forward in his hand, and the blade caught the starlight and flashed silver.

"Ahhhh...so you would fight?"

"I...just want to go," he said. He felt one of the weapons behind prick through his shirt, and jerked forward, away from that pain. The shadows in front retreated, as if that knife were a real weapon. He waved it experimentally, and they flinched away.

"Do you know what you bear?" the voice asked.

"It's a knife," he said.

"Thou art a fool, mortal man," the voice said. "Stay away from our highways; thy luck may change." The pricks at his side and back vanished; a huddle of dark shapes ran together, vanishing into the tunnel beneath the grass.

Dall stood up, his heart pounding. He could see nothing across the field but a blurred line where he had come from, his body pushing the grass and flowers aside, but nothing ahead. Yet now he knew the footpath was perilous, he could not go back to it. He did not know what those beings were. He never wanted to see them again.

From the line of his passage the day before, he struck out at an angle, pushing his way through the waist-high growth. As anyone who has ever tried it, he found walking in the dark more difficult than he expected. Where the surface of the flowers seemed level, the land below dipped and rose beneath his feet, here a hummock like a miniature hill just high enough to catch his toe, and there a hollow deep enough to jar his teeth when he staggered into it. He pushed on, careless of the noise he made and any hazards he might wake, until—witless with fatigue— he caught his foot on yet another hummock and measured his length in the tall growth, falling hard enough to knock the breath from his lungs. And there he slept, overcome by all that had happened, until the sun rose and an early bee buzzed past his ear.

In the morning, he could scarcely understand his panic of the night. He stood, stretched, and looked around him. His backward path was clear, a trampled line that twisted and turned like that of a fleeing rabbit. He thought he had gone straight, but by day he could see that he had not come half so far from the…the highway…as he hoped.

Remembering that, he looked again at his sister's gift. Clearly wood, carved to the likeness of a knife, and polished. In the low slanting light, he could see the incised design he'd felt before. He ran his forefinger over it, but nothing happened, and the lines themselves meant nothing to him. Whatever it was, it had driven away those…whatever they were.

He was hungry, but he often woke hungry at home, and nothing to eat until chores were done. He was thirsty, but he would come to water soon; all he had to do was go on. He looked around at the wide, green, flower-spangled world, and saw nothing he knew. He told himself he was happy about that. No father and brothers to bully him; no sisters to scold and laugh.

As morning wore on, hunger and thirst vied for his attention. Thirst won; by afternoon, he could think of nothing but water... and no water could he see, or sign of it. No friendly line of trees beside a brook or river...all around the grass lifted and flattened in the wind, billowing...the hills as distant as ever, flat and shimmery against the pale sky. He went on, into the lowering sun, hoping to get to the hills...surely he would find trees and water there.

Instead, he trod on something that yielded beneath his foot, and sharp pain stabbed his leg. With a gasp and cry, he threw himself away from whatever it was, and caught a glimpse of a long, sinuous body, checkered brown and yellow, as he landed hard on his side. He scrambled to his feet, but whatever it had been did not follow him. His leg burned and throbbed; the pain ran up and down his leg like scalding water. Groaning, he sat down again, and pulled up his trews. Two tiny dark holes a thumbwidth apart, and a rapidly purpling bruise around them. He felt sick and shaky. It must have been a serpent, but the little grass and water snakes near home had been smaller. They never bit anyone—of course he'd never stepped on one...

Suddenly his mouth was full of sour mucus; he spat, and blinked away tears. Poison. It was some kind of poison. His mother's mother, before she died, had said something about poison from evil creatures. Cut it out, she'd said, or cut it off. The wooden knife could not be sharp or strong enough, but it was all he had.

He touched the point of it to one of the fang-marks, but he could not make himself push it in...the pain was already beyond bearing, and how could he cause more. Thick yellow ooze came from the wound, running down over his leg like honey. He stared, blinked, and realized he felt better. The flow of liquid stopped.

He moved the knife point to the other fang-mark, holding his breath...and again, the thick yellow oozed out, ran down his leg. His belly steadied back to the simple ache of hunger; his mouth was dry again. As he watched, the fang-mark closed over, leaving a dry pale dimple. The other one still gaped; he moved the knife tip back to it, and it too closed over.

Grass rustled; he jerked up, stared. Unwinking eyes stared at him from a narrow head on a long, coiled body. Another serpent, this one much larger. A pink forked tongue flickered out; he flinched, scooting backwards, and held the knife forward. The serpent's head lowered.

Slowly, trembling, he clambered to his feet. He wanted to back away but what if there was another one...? Holding the knife toward the serpent, he dared a quick glance behind him.

At his back stood someone he had never seen, someone who had appeared...he almost forgot the serpent, in that astonishment, but the serpent moved, and that caught his eye. Slowly, without appearing to move at all, it lowered its coils until it lay flat to the ground, and then, too fast to follow, whipped about and vanished into the grass.

"You're very lucky," the person said.

Dall could say nothing. He shook his head a little in his confusion. How could a full-grown man, dressed in fine leathers and a shirt with a lace collar, and boots to the thigh, have walked up on him without making a noise?

"I surprised you," the person said. "As you surprised the serpent's child."

"I don't know you," Dall said. He could think of nothing else to say.

"Nor I you," the stranger said. "But it needs no names to befriend someone, does it?"

"I—I'm Dall," Dall said. He almost added *Gory the Tall's third son*, but didn't because he had left home and could no longer claim his father's name.

"And I am Verthan," the stranger said. "You're a long way from a village, Dall. Gone hunting a lost sheep?"

"No...I left home," Dall said.

"You travel light," the stranger—Verthan—said. "Most men setting out would take at least a waterskin."

"Didn't have one," Dall muttered.

"Then you're thirsty, surely," Verthan said. "Have a drink of mine." He unhooked from his belt a skin dyed scarlet, bound in brown.

Dall reached for it, his mouth suddenly dryer than ever, but then pulled his hand back. He had nothing to trade, nothing at all, and the deepest rule he knew was hearth-sharing. He shook his head and shrugged.

"Nothing to share? You must have left in a hurry." Verthan shook his head. "You've set yourself a hard road, lad. But you'll not go much farther without water—water you must have."

Dall felt the words as if they were a hot summer wind in the hayfield; he felt dryness reach down his throat to his very marrow.

"I'll tell you what," Verthan said. "Why not trade your knife? Come evening, if you'll travel with me, we'll come to a place where you can gather early fruits, and we can trade it back to you. How's that?" He held out the water skin. Dall could see the damp surface of it; he could almost smell the water inside it; he could certainly hear it as the man shook it.

His hand jerked, as if someone had caught it from behind, and he felt the edges of the knife against the insides of his clenched fingers. The memory of the snake venom oozing out, and the sickness leaving...the memory of Julya's face, as she handed him the knife… He shook his head, mute because his mouth was too dry to speak.

Verthan's expression sharpened into anger, then relaxed again into humor. "You are not as stupid as you look," he said. Then, as wind blows a column of smoke, he blew away, and where he had stood a rustle in the grass moved off downslope.

Dall's knees loosened and he slumped down into the grass, frightened as he was of the grass and all that lived in it. He sat huddled a long time, hardly even aware of his thirst and hunger, while fear fled ice-cold up and down his veins.

Some while later, when fear had worn itself out, he became aware of something wet touching his hand. Too tired now to jump away, he looked. The wooden knife in his heart-hand, blunt as it was, had poked a little way through the grass stems into the soil beneath. The wet soil, he now saw, for the base of the grass stems around it glistened with water, and his hand and the knife.

At once his thirst returned, fierce as fire, and he scrabbled at the place, digging with the knife. He could see it, he could smell it…when he had opened a space the size of his cupped palm, he pushed his face into it and a sucked in a half-mouthful of water flavored with shreds of dry grass and dirt. He spat out the mud, and swallowed the scant water. The tiny pool refilled; he drank again, this time with less mud in his mouth. Again. Again. And again. Each a scant mouthful, but each restoring a little of his strength.

When he had drunk until he could hold no more, he sat up and looked again at his sister's gift. Through his mind ran the events since he'd left home—the attack of the little people, the snakes, the phantom of the air, his thirst. Each time the thing had saved him, and he did not understand how. It looked like something an idle boy might whittle from any handy stick of wood. He himself had no skill at carving, but he had seen such things, little wooden animals and people and swords. As far as he knew—which seemed less far than the day before—none of those were magical. And so…his mind moved slowly, carefully, along the unaccustomed paths of logic…this must not be what it looked like. It must be something else. But what?

By now the sun hung low over the hills. He looked around. He had no idea where to go, or how to avoid the dangers he now knew inhabited these apparently harmless meadows. Only the gift that had saved him…could it help him find his way?

He bent again to the tiny pool of water, and then stood, holding the knife as always in his heart hand. How could he tell it his need? His hand twitched, without his intention. The thought came into his mind that he had not needed to tell the knife what his need was before. He held out his hand, palm up, and opened it. The knife squirmed on his hand—he almost dropped it in a moment of panic—and the tip pointed the way he least expected, downslope and back the way he had come. Toward that perilous footpath. Even—if he thought about it—toward home.

He did not want to go that way. Surely, with the knife's help, he could go on the way he wanted, into the hills…he might find more dangers, but the knife would protect him. It might even feed him.

His hand fell with the sudden weight of the knife, and lost its grip; the knife disappeared into the tall grass.

Dall cried out, wordless surprise and fear, and threw himself into the grass, feeling among the springy stems for something stiff, unyielding, wooden. Nothing. He tried to unthink the thought he'd had, promising the thing that he would follow its guidance always, in everything, if it would only come back.

Always? The question hung in the air, unspoken by mortal

voice, but ringing in Dall's ears like the blow of a hammer.

"I'm sorry," he muttered aloud. "Julya gave it to me, and she loved me…"

A gust of wind flattened the grass over his head; pollen stung his eyes. He turned to blink and clear them, and there it lay, on top of the grass he had flattened while sitting on it. He reached out gingerly, wondering if it would let him touch it, and picked it up.

No heavier than at first. No less plain wood than at first. It lay motionless in his hand and when he stood he was facing the way the blade had pointed.

"All right then," he said. "Show me."

With water enough in his belly, the worst of the day's heat past, and the sun and high ground behind him, he made quick progress down and across the slope. Now his feet found good purchase wherever he trod, now the wind at his back cooled him without burning his face.

In the last of the light, he came to a stream fringed with trees. Was it the same stream he had crossed at the ford near his home? He could not tell, in the gloom. The knife had led him between the fringing trees to a flat rock beside the water, and there he drank his fill again, and there he found ready to hand the green leaves he knew could be eaten safely. He fell asleep on the rock, warded on three sides by clean running water, and woke before dawn, cold and stiff but otherwise unharmed, the knife still in his hand.

He expected the knife to lead him back home, to return it to his sister Julya, but instead it led him upstream, and insisted (for its guidance strengthened as the day went on) that he stay within the trees beside the stream, and on this hither side. Because of the trees, he could not see the land around, but he knew it rose by the ache in his legs from climbing, always climbing, ever more steeply as the water's note changed from the quiet gurgle lower down to the high, rapid laugh as it fell over taller and taller rocks.

Near the stream he found a few early berries, gleaming red, and ate them, along with more of the greens. He pried loose a few clingshells from rocks and sucked out the sweet meat inside; he managed to tickle one fish in the noon silence, when the knife had made it clear (how he was still not sure) that he should rest by the stream awhile. Always he had water to drink, so by nightfall he was well content to sleep again, this time in a hollow between oak roots.

Midmorning the next day, following the stream ever higher, he came out of the woods into a wide bare land of low grass, with here and there tussocks of reeds and an occasional gnarled shrub. Now he could see over the land—see how the trees traced out the stream below in its twists and turns and joinings with others… see little columns of smoke far in the distance that might have come from farmhouse chimneys…see the great green sea of grass breaking on the hills' knees, washing up this high as grass that would not cover the top of his foot.

Upslope, where the stream leaped in silver torrents from rock to rock, the land heaped up in mounds as far as he could see, all the way to the pale sky. Off to his right a great rocky wall, blue-shadowed and white-topped, had risen as if from nowhere… far higher than the hills he'd seen from home.

You wanted adventure. Again that voiceless voice, those words with no breath, hung in the air. *Now will you follow? Or shall I take you home?*

Against the memory of home—sweeter now than it had been when he left—came the memory of that first night and day of terror, and then the pleasanter but still strenuous days of travel since. What finally determined him to keep going was the memory of Julya. She would be glad to see him come home, but she alone had believed he might do something…become something. For her he would keep going until he could bring her…something worth the gift she had given him.

"I'll go on," Dall said.

Silence. He scrubbed one leg with the other foot, and waited. The knife lay quiescent in his hand. That had not, he realized, been the question. It had been *follow or go home*, not *go on or go home*.

"I'll follow," he said.

The knife twitched, and Dall headed on up the steepening slope, following the knife and the cold rush of water.

Finally, legs trembling with fatigue, he staggered up yet another slope to find that the water gushed from a cleft in the rocks beside the thread of trail. Above him the slope broke into vertical slabs of rock, bare and forbidding in the evening shadows beneath a darkening sky. Dall looked back, where the land beyond sloped down again, down and down into a purple gloom that hid every place he had ever been. Did the knife expect him to climb those rocks? He was sure he could not. He looked around for someplace to sleep, finally creeping between two massive boulders each bigger than his family's hut, but an insistent breeze chilled him wherever he tried to curl up, and he could not really sleep.

He was awake, and just this side of shivering in the chill, when he heard the cry. He was on his feet, peering wide-eyed into the darkness, when he felt the knife twitch in his hand. "But it's dark," he said. "I can't see where I'm going." He thought perhaps the knife would glow, giving light for him to see. Instead, it pricked his fingers, a sharp sting.

Another cry, and hoarse shouts. Shaking with fear, Dall started that way, only to run into one of the rocks. He scrabbled back; his foot landed on loose rubble, and he fell, rocks rolling about him and down below, loud and louder. He slid with them, flung out his arms and tried to stop himself. He had scrambled up over a ledge...and now his legs waved in the cold air, his belly lay against a sharp irregular edge, his bruised, skinned fingers dug in.

He pulled himself up a little, panting with fear, and felt around with his use-hand for a better purchase. Then his foot bumped the rock below, and he remembered where the foothold had been. He let himself slide backwards, into the air and darkness, and another rock fell from the ledge, bounced loudly below, and hit something that clanged louder than his mother's soup-kettle.

This time he heard, though he did not understand the words, the angry voice below. He pressed himself against the cold rock, shivering. But his heart-hand cramped, and he had to move, and again rocks fell from under his feet, and he lost his grip on the rock, falling his own length in a rattle of small stones to land on something that heaved and swore, this time in words he'd heard before. Hard hands clamped on his bare ankle, on his arm, angry voices swore revenge and stank of bad ale and too much onion...and without thought his heart-hand swept forward, and the hand on his ankle released it with a hiss of pain, and with another swipe the grip on his arm disappeared.

"Back!" he heard someone say, panting. "It's not worth it—" And there was a scramble and rattle and clang and clatter of rocks on stone, and metal on rocks, and shod feet on rocks and someone falling and someone cursing—more than one someone—all drawing away into the night and leaving him crouched breathless and shaking.

He drew a long breath and let it out in a sigh that was almost a sob. Like an echo of his own, another sigh followed, then a groan. He froze, staring into darkness, seeing nothing…he could hear breathing. Harsh, irregular, with a little grunt at each exhalation. Off to his left a little, the way the knife pulled at him now. He took a cautious step, his left foot landing on a sharp pebble—a quick step then, and his foot came down on something soft, yielding.

The scream that followed knocked him to the ground like a blow, his fear came so strongly. Once there he fell asleep all at once, heedless of his scrapes and bruises and the danger.

* * *

In the first cold light of dawn, the man's face might have been carved of the stone he lay on, flesh tight to the bone with care and pain. Dall stared at the face. Longer of jaw than his father's, it still had something of the same look in the deep lines beside the mouth, the deep-cut furrows of the brow.

Color seeped into the world with the light. That dark stain, almost black at first, was blood—bright red where it was new, the color of dirty rust where it had dried. The man's shirt had once been white, and edged with lace; now it was filthy, soaked with blood, spattered with it even where it was not soaked. His trews were cut differently than any Dall had seen, fitted closer to his legs, and he had boots—real leather boots—on his feet. They were caked with dried mud, worn at the instep, with scuffed marks on the side of the heels. The dangling ends of thongs at his waist showed where something had been cut away. Dall could smell the blood, and the sour stench of ale as well.

The man groaned. Dall shuddered. He knew nothing of healing arts, and surely the man was dying. Dead men—men dead of violence, and not eased into the next world by someone who knew the right words to say—could not rest. Their angry spirits rose from their bodies and sought unwary travelers whose souls eased their hunger and left the travelers their helpless slaves forever. Such tales Dall's grandda had told by the winter fireside; Dall knew he was in danger more than mortal, for he knew none of the right words to smooth a dying man's path.

He tried to push himself up, but he was too stiff to stand up and his ankle—he could just see, now, that it was swollen as big as a cabbage and he could feel it throbbing—would not bear his weight even as he tried to get away on hands and knees.

The man shifted in his blood-soaked clothes, groaned again, and opened his eyes. Dall stared. Bloodshot green eyes stared back.

"Holy Falk," the man said. His voice was breathy but firm, not the voice of a dying man. He sounded more annoyed than anything else. He glanced down at himself and grimaced. "What happened, boy?"

Dall gulped, swallowed, and spoke aloud for the first time in days. "I don't know…sir."

"Ah…my head…" The man lay back, closed his eyes a moment, and then looked at Dall again. "Bring water, there's a good lad, and some bread…"

The incongruity made Dall giggle with relief. The man scowled.

"There's no bread," Dall said. His stomach growled loudly at that. "And I don't have a waterskin."

"Am I not in the sotyard…?" The man pushed himself up on one elbow, and his brows raised. "No, I suppose I'm not. What place is this, boy?"

"I don't know, sir." This time the *sir* had come easily.

"Are you lost too, then?"

"I—aren't you dying, then?"

The man laughed, a laugh that caught on a groan. "No, boy. Not that easily. Why did you think—?" He looked down at himself, and muttered "Blood...always blood..." then squeezed his eyes shut and shook his head. When he next looked up, his face was different somehow. "Look here, boy, I hear a stream. You could at least fetch some water from there...I have a waterskin..." He patted his sides, then shook his head. "Or I suppose I don't. It must've been thieves, I imagine. Were there thieves, boy?"

"I didn't see them," Dall said. Odds on this man was a thief himself. "I heard yells in the dark. Then I fell..."

Now the man's eyes looked at him as if really seeing him. "By the gods, you did fall—you look almost as bad as I feel. You saved my life," the man said. "It was a brave thing, to come down on unknown dangers in the dark, and take on two armed men, a boy like you."

Dall felt his ears going hot. "I...didn't mean to," he said.

"Didn't mean to?"

"No...I fell off the cliff."

"Still, your fall saved me, I don't doubt. Ohhhh..." Another groan, and the man had pushed himself up to sitting, and grabbed for his head as if it would fall off and roll away. "I don't know why I drink that poison they call ale..."

"For the comfort of forgetting," Dall said, quoting his father.

A harsh laugh answered him. "Aye, that's the truth, though you're over-young to have anything worth forgetting, I'd say. You—" The man stopped suddenly and stared at the ground by Dall's hand. "Where did you get that?" he asked.

Dall had forgotten the knife, but there it lay, glinting a little in first rays of the sun. He reached and put his hand over it. "My sister gave it to me," he said. "It's only wood…"

"I see that," the man said. He shook his head, and then grunted with pain. Dall knew that sound; his father had been drunk every quarter-day as long as he could remember. The man pushed himself to hands and knees, and crawled to the tiny stream, where he drank, and splashed water on himself, and then, standing, stripped off his bloody clothes. There was plenty of light now, and Dall could see the bruises and cuts on skin like polished ivory, marked as it was with old scars on his sides.

While the man's back was turned, Dall pushed himself up a little, wincing at the pain—he hurt everywhere—and picked up the wooden knife. If it could mend a serpent bite, what about a swollen ankle? And for that matter the bloody scrape some rock had made along his arm? He laid the knife to his arm, but nothing happened. Nor when he touched it to his ankle.

The man turned around while Dall still had the knife on his ankle. "What are you doing?" he asked sharply.

"Nothing," Dall said, pulling his hand back quickly. "Just seeing how bad it hurt if I touched it."

"Hmmm." The man cocked his head. "You know, boy—what is your name, anyway?"

"Dall Drop—Dall, son of Gory," Dall said.

"Dall Drop? That's one I haven't heard."

"My father calls me 'Drop-hand'," Dall said, ducking his head.

"Drop-*body*, if last night was any example," the man said, chuckling. Dall felt himself going hot. "Nay, boy—it's not so bad. Your dropping in no doubt scared those thieves away. Maybe it was all accident, but you did good by it. Let's see about your wounds…"

"They're not wounds," Dall said. "Just cuts and things."

"Well, cuts or whatever, they could use some healing," the man said. He looked around. "And none of the right herbs here. We'll have to get you down to a wood, and you can't walk on that ankle."

"'M sorry," Dall muttered.

"Nonsense," the man said. "Just let me get the blood off this—" He took his wadded shirt back to the creek. Dall gaped. Was he going to pollute the pure water with his blood? But the man sat down, pulled off one of his boots, and scooped up a bootful of water, then stuffed his shirt into the boot and shook it vigorously. The water came out pink; he dumped the wet shirt on the ground, emptied the bloody water into a clump of grass, and did it again. That was bad enough, but at least he wasn't dipping the shirt itself in the water.

After several changes of water, he came back to Dall with the sopping mess of his shirt, wrung it out, and reached for Dall's foot. "This'll hurt, boy, but it'll help, too."

It did hurt; every movement of the foot hurt, and the wet shirt was icy. The man wrapped it around his ankle, and used the sleeves to tie it tightly. Dall could feel his bloodbeat throbbing against the tight wrapping.

"Now, boy, give me your hand."

Dall had reached out his hand before he thought; the man took it and heaved him up in one movement.

"You'll have to walk; I'm still too drunk to carry you safely on this ground," the man said. "I can help, though. Let me guide you."

"Sir," Dall said. His foot hurt less than he expected as he hobbled slowly, leaning on the man's shoulder. The other aches also subsided with movement, though his cuts and scrapes stung miserably.

It was a slow, painful traverse of the slope, down and across, even when they came to the thread of a path the man said he'd followed the night before. "Sheep are not men," the man said, when they came to the first drop in the path. He slid down first, and Dall followed. The man caught him before his bad ankle hit the path. That was almost all the man said, other than the occasional "Mind this" and "That rock tips."

The sun was high overhead when the path widened abruptly at the head of a grassy valley, where several sheep trails came together. Ahead, smoke rose from a huddle of low buildings. Dall could smell cooked food for the first time in days; his stomach growled again and he felt suddenly faint. He sagged; the man muttered something but took more of his weight. "Come on, boy—you've done well so far," he said.

Dall blinked and gulped, and managed to stand more on his own feet. The man helped him down the wider track to an open space where someone had placed a couple of rough benches around a firepit. No one was visible outside the buildings, but from the smell someone was busy inside them. The man lowered Dall to one of them, then bent to unwrap his ankle. "I need a shirt, boy, if I'm to talk someone into giving us food. And down here I should be able to find the right leaves for your injuries."

Dall's ankle had turned unlovely shades of green and purple; now his foot was swollen as well. The man shrugged into the wet, dirty shirt, and headed for one of the huts as if he knew it. Dall glanced around, and caught sight of someone peeking around a house-wall at him. A child, younger, smaller. He looked away, then looked back quickly. A boy, wearing a ragged shirt much like his own over short trews…barefoot as he was. The boy offered a shy smile; Dall smiled back. The boy came nearer; he could have been Dall's younger brother if he'd had one.

"What happened to you?" the boy asked. "Did he beat you?"

"No," Dall said. "I fell on the mountain."

"You need to wrap that," the boy said, pointing to his ankle. "Are you hungry?"

"I have nothing to share," Dall said.

"You're hurt. It's Lady's grace," the boy said. "Don't you have that where you come from?"

"Yes...I just..."

"I'll get something," the boy said, and was gone like a minnow in the stream, in an instant.

He was back in a moment, with a hunk of bread in his hand. "Here, traveler; may the Lady's grace nourish us both."

"In grace given, in grace eaten, blessed be the Lady." Dall broke the bread, giving a piece back to the boy, and looked around for the man. He had disappeared; an empty doorway suggested where he'd gone. Dall took a bite of bread and the younger boy did also.

Bread tasted better than anything he'd ever eaten, so much better that he forgot the pain in his foot, and his other pains. He could've eaten the whole piece, but he set aside a careful half for the man, in case no one shared with him.

But the man was coming back now, carrying a jug and another loaf. "I see you've made friends," he said.

"I saved you a bit," Dall said. "It's Lady's grace."

The man raised his eyebrows. "I suppose we could all use grace." He ate the piece Dall had set aside, then broke the loaf he carried. "Here—you could eat more, I daresay. And here's water."

Dall wanted to ask if this too had been given as Lady's grace, but he didn't. The man sat a few minutes, eating, and taking sips of the water. Then he stood. "I'd best be going to work," he said. "There's a wall to mend." He nodded at the far end of the village, where one wall of a sheepfold bulged out, missing stones at the top. Dall started to push himself up and the man shook his head. "Not you, boy. You're still hurt. Just rest there, and one of the women will be out to tend you shortly. She's boiling water for boneset tea for you."

That night Dall lay on straw, his injured ankle wrapped in old rags. Sleeping under a roof again after so many nights in the open made him as wakeful as his first nights on the trail. He could hear the breathing of others in the cottage, and smell them all too. He wanted to crawl outside into the clean night air scented with growing things, but that would be rude. Finally he fell asleep, and the next morning ate his porridge with pleasure. Cooked food was worth the discomforts of the night, he decided.

He and the man stayed in the village for six hands of days; the man worked at whatever chores anyone put him to, without comment or complaint. As Dall became able to hobble around more easily, he too worked. It was strange to do the familiar work he had grown up with, but for strangers. When he dropped something—less often than before—he waited for the familiar jibes, but none came. Not even when he dropped a jug of new milk and broke the jug.

"Never mind," said the woman for whom he'd been carrying that jug and two others. "It's my fault for giving you more than you could carry, and the handle on that one's been tricky for years." She was a cheerful dark-haired woman with wide hips and a wider smile; all her children were like her, and the boy who had first given him bread was her youngest.

One evening after supper, Dall had an itch down his back, and scratched at it with the point of the wooden knife. The man watched him, and then asked, "Where did you get that knife?"

"I told you—my sister gave it to me." Dall sighed with relief as the tip found the perfect itchy spot to scratch.

"And where did she get it?"

"She found it in the woods last fall; we were all out nutting together, and she was feeling among the leaves in between the roots, and there it was."

"By itself?"

"I don't know. I didn't see her find it. Why, what could have been with it?"

The man sat down, heavily. "Dall, I carved that knife myself, two winters gone. I had thrown away my sword—oh, aye, I had a sword once, and mail that shone like silver, and a fine prancing horse, too. I had a dagger yet, and while I was snowed in, that first winter of my freedom, I whittled away on the kindling sticks. Most I burnt, but a few I kept, for the pleasure of remembering my boy's skill. Then spring came, and when I set out again I tossed them in the stream one summer's day to watch them float away."

"So the knife is yours," Dall said.

"I threw it away," the man said. "Like my sword. And unlike my sword it has come back, in a hand that valued it more." He cleared his throat. "I just wondered...if any of the others were found. Some flowers—mostly rose designs, over and over—and one fairly good horse."

"I don't know," Dall said. "But if the knife is yours..." He held it out.

The man shook his head. "No, lad. I threw it away; it's yours now."

"But it's special," Dall said. "It saved me—" He rattled on quickly, sensing the man's unwillingness to hear, about the little people in the grass, and the serpent's bite, and the strange being that appeared from nowhere and vanished back into nowhere, and the water…

The man stared at him, open-mouthed. "That knife?"

"This knife," Dall said. He held it out again. "Your knife. You made it; the magic must be from you."

"'To ward from secret treachery, from violence and from guile, from deadly thirst and hunger, from evil creatures vile…'" The man's voice trailed off. "It can't be…" His fingers stretched toward it, then his fist clenched. "It can't be. It's gone; what's loosed cannot be caught again."

"That's silly," Dall said. He felt silly too, holding out the knife. "When we let the calf out of the pen, we just catch it and bring it back."

"Magic is not a cow, boy!" The man's voice was hoarse now; Dall hardly dared look at his face for the anger he expected to see, but instead there were tears running down the furrows beside his mouth. "I forswore it…"

And will the wind not blow? And will not the spring return? The man's head jerked up; he must have heard it too.

Dall took a small step forward, and laid the knife in the man's hand, folding the man's fingers around it. As he stepped back, he saw the change, as if the sun had come out from behind a cloud. Light washed over the man, and behind it the man's filthy old shirt shone whiter than any cloth Dall had seen. His scuffed, worn boots gleamed black; his mud-streaked trews were spotless. On his tired, discouraged face, a new expression came: hope, and love, and light. What had seemed gray hair, once clean, now gleamed a healthy brown.

And the knife, the simple wooden knife, stretched and changed, until the man held a sword out of old tales. Dall had never seen a sword at all, let alone such a sword as that.

Vows are not so easily broken, or duties laid aside. Dall had no idea what that was about, but the man did; his quick head-shake and shrug changed to an expression of mingled awe and sorrow. He fell to his knees, holding the sword carefully, hilt upright. Dall backed away; a stone nudged the back of his legs and he sat down on it. He watched the man's lips move silently, until the man looked straight at him out of those strange green eyes, eyes still bright with tears.

"Well, boy, you have done quite a work here."

"I didn't mean to," Dall said.

"I'm glad you did," the man said. He stood, and held out his hand. "Come, let me call you friend. My name's Felis, and I was once a paladin of Falk. It seems Falk wants me back, even after— even now." He looked at the sword, the corners of his mouth quirking up in what was not quite a smile. "I think I'd better find this wood where your sister found the knife I carved, and see if any of the other bits washed up there. Something tells me the road back to Falk may prove...interesting."

Dall took the proffered hand and stood.

"What about me?" he asked.

"I hope you will travel with me," the man said. "You saved my life and you brought me back my knife...my life, actually, as a servant of Falk. And surely you want the sister who found it to know that it saved you."

"Go *home*?" Dall's voice almost squeaked. He could imagine his father's sarcasm, his brother's blows.

"It seems we both must," Felis said. "We both ran away; the knife called us both. But neither of us will stay with your father, I'm sure. What—do you think a boy who has saved a paladin remains a drop-hand forever?"

* * *

In the days of high summer, when the trees stood sentinel over their shade at noon, still and watchful, and spring's racing waters had quieted to clear pools and murmuring riffles, Dall no longer Drop-hand returned to his home, walking across the hayfield with a tall man whose incongruous clothes bore no sweat-stains, even in that heat. Gory the Tall recognized Dall the moment he came out of the trees, but the man with the spotless white shirt and the sword he did not recognize. Dall's brothers stood as if struck by lightning, watching their brother come, moving with the grace of one who does not stumble even on rough paths.

That evening, in the long soft twilight, Felis told of Dall's courage, of the magic in the knife he'd carved, of his oaths and his need to return.

"Then—I suppose this is yours too," said the youngest girl, Julya. She fished out of her bodice a little flat circle of wood carved with rose petals and held it out to him. Dall could hear the tears in her voice.

Felis shook his head. "Nay, lass. When I carved the flowers, I thought of my own sisters, far away. If it has magic, let it comfort you." He touched it with his finger. Then the air was filled with the perfume of roses, a scent that faded only slowly. The girl's face glowed with joy; she sniffed it again and tucked it back into her clothes.

"And he really saved you?" Dall's oldest brother asked.

"I slipped and fell," Dall said.

"At exactly the right moment," Felis said, a wave of his hand shutting off the gibes Dall's brothers had ready. "I hope he'll come with me, help me find the rest of the carvings I must find before I go back to my order."

"But—" Gory the Tall peered through the gloom at his son and at Felis. "If he's not the boy he was…"

"Then it's time for him to leave," Felis said. He turned to Dall. "If you want to, that is."

He was home without blows and jeers; he had triumphed. If he stayed, he would have that to fall back on. Stories to tell, scars to show. If he left, this time it would be for such adventures as paladins find—he knew far more about real adventures now than he had...and he was no longer angry and hurt, with every reason to go and none to stay.

An evening breeze stirred the dust, waking all the familiar smells of home. At his back, Julya pressed close; he could just smell the rose-scent of the carving in her bodice. But beyond that, he could smell the creek, the trees, the indefinable scent of lands beyond that he had only begun to know.

"I will go with you," he said to Felis. And then, to his family, "And someday I will come home again, with gifts for you all."

The End

AUTHOR'S NOTE ON
FIRST BLOOD

Luden Fall, great-nephew of the Duke of Fall in this story contemporaneous with events in *Crown of Renewal*, is not in the direct line of succession for any title. He did not expect to be sent out with a troop of cavalry as the representative of the family, off to the northwest to keep watch on the road along the foot of the Dwarfmounts. Everyone knows the invasion will come from the south, so he suspects he was sent away just to keep him safely away from battle. Only his older cousins will have a chance at glory. But war defies predictions, and so does Luden.

Publication note: "First Blood" was originally published in *Shattered Shields*, Baen Books, ed. Jennifer Brozek & Bryan Thomas Schmidt, 2014.

First Blood

Luden Fall, great-nephew of the Duke Of Fall, had not won the spurs he strapped to his boots the morning he left home for the first time. War had come to Fallo, so Luden, three years too young for knighthood, had been given the honor of accompanying a cohort of Sofi Ganarrion's company to represent the family.

The cohort's captain, Madrelar, a lean, angular man with a weathered, sun-browned face, eyed him up and down and then shrugged. "We march in a ladyglass," Madrelar said. "There's your horse. Get your gear tied on and be at my side when we mount up."

The mounted troop moved quickly, riding longer and faster than Luden had before, into territory he had never seen, ever closer to the Dwarfmounts that divided the Eight Kingdoms of the North from Aarenis. His duties were minimal. When he first attempted to help the way he'd been taught at home, picking up and putting in place everything the captain put down, carrying dishes to and from a serving table, Madrelar told him to quit fussing about. Luden obeyed, as squires were supposed to do.

He had hoped to learn much from a mercenary captain, a man who had fought against Siniava and might have seen the Duke of Immer when he was still Alured the Black and an ally, but Madrelar said little to him beyond simple orders and discouraged questions by not answering them. Pastak, the cohort sergeant, said less. The troopers themselves ignored him, though he heard mutters and chuckles he assumed were at his expense.

Finally one evening, when the sentries were out walking the bounds, the captain called Luden into his tent. "You should know where we are and why," Madrelar said. He had maps spread on a folding table. "We guard the North Trade Road, where the road from Rotengre meets it, so Immer cannot outflank the duke's force. It's unlikely he'll try, but just in case. Do you understand?"

Luden looked at the map, at the captain's finger pointing to a crossroads. Back there was Fallo, where he had lived all his life until now. "Yes," he said. "I understand outflanking, and I can see…" He traced the line with his finger. "They could come this way, along the north road. But could they not also follow the route we took here, only bypassing us to the south?"

"They are unlikely to know the way," Madrelar said.

"What force might they bring?" Luden asked.

Madrelar shrugged. "Anything from nothing to five hundred. If they are too large, we retreat, sending word back for reinforcements. If they are small enough, we destroy them. In the middle…" He tipped his hand back and forth. "We fight and see who wins." He gave Luden a sharp glance out of frosty blue eyes. "Are you scared, boy?"

"Not really." Luden's skin prickled, but he knew it for excitement, not fear.

Madrelar grinned. "That will change."

The next day they stayed in camp. Madrelar told him to take all three of the captain's mounts to be checked for loose shoes. Luden waited his turn for the farrier, listening to the men talk, hoping to hear stories of Siniava's War. Instead, the men talked of drinking, dicing, money, women, and when they would be back in "a real city."

"Sorellin?" Luden asked, having seen that it was nearest on the map.

They all stopped and looked at him, then at one another. Finally one of them said, "No, young lord. Valdaire. Have you heard of it?"

"Of course—it's in the west, near the caravan pass to the north."

"It's *our* city," the man said. "Any other place we go, we're on hire. But in Valdaire, we're free."

"The girls in Valdaire..." another man said, making shapes with his hands. "They love us, for we bring money."

Luden felt his ears getting hot. His own interest in girls was new, and his father's lectures on deportment both clear and stringent.

"Don't embarrass the lad," the first trooper said. "He'll find out in time." His glance quieted the others. "You ride well, young lord. It is an honor to have a member of your family along."

"Thank you," Luden said. He knew the other men were amused, but this one seemed polite. "My name is Luden. This is the first time I have been so far."

Silence for a moment, then the man said, "I am Esker." He gestured. "These are Trongar, Vesk, and Hrondar. We all came south from Kostandan with Ganarrion."

Luden fizzed with questions he wanted to ask—was the north really all forest? Was it true that elves walked there? Esker tipped his head toward the fire. "Janits waits you and the captain's horses. Best go, or someone will take your place in line."

"Thank you," Luden said, and led the horses forward.

* * *

When he returned the horses to the hitch-line strung between trees, it was still broad daylight. He glanced in the captain's tent—orderly and empty. The men were busy with camp chores, with horse care, cleaning tack, mending anything that needed it. Luden's own small possessions were new enough to need nothing.

Luden spoke to the nearest sentry. "Would it be all right if I went for a walk?"

The man's brows rose. "You think that's a good idea? You do realize there might be an enemy army not a day's march away?"

"I thought...nothing's happening...I could just look at things."

The sentry heaved a dramatic sigh. "All right. Don't go far, don't get hurt, if you see strangers, come back and tell me. All right? Back in one sun-hand, no more."

"Thank you," Luden said. He looked around for a moment, thinking which way to go. Little red dots on a bush a stone's throw away caught his eye.

The dots were indeed berries, some ripened to purple, but most still red and sour. Luden ate some of the ripe ones, and brought a neck-cloth full back to the camp. At home, the cooks were always happy to get berries, however few. Here, too, the camp cook nodded when Luden offered them. "Can you get more?"

"I think so," Luden said.

"Take this bowl. Be back in..." he glanced up at the sun, "a sun-hand, and I'll be able to use these for dinner."

Luden showed the sentry the bowl. "Cook wants more of those berries."

"Good," the sentry said.

Near the first bush were others; Luden filled the bowl and

took it back to the cook. After that—still no sign of the captain—Luden wandered about the camp until he found Esker, the man who had been friendly before, replacing a strap on a saddle.

"If you've nothing to do, you can punch some holes in this strap," Esker said.

Luden sat down at once. Esker handed him another strap and the punching tools, and told him how to space the holes. Luden soon made a row of neat holes. "Good job, lad—Luden, wasn't it? Have you checked all your own tack?"

"It's almost new," Luden said. "I didn't see anything wrong."

"Bring it here. We'll give you a lesson in field maintenance of cavalry tack."

Luden brought his saddle, bridle, and rigging over to Esker where he sat amid a group of busy troopers. Luden had cleaned his tack, but—as Esker pointed out—he hadn't gone over every finger-width of every strap.

"You might think this doesn't matter as much," Hrondar said. Esker's friends had now joined in the instruction. Hrondar pointed to the strap that held a water bottle on his own saddle. "If that gives way and you have no water on a long march, you'll be less alert. Everything we carry is needed. Every strap should be checked daily to see it's not cracked, drying out, stretching too much."

Other men shared their ideas for keeping tack in perfect condition—including arguments about the best oils and waxes for different weather. Luden drank it in, fascinated by details his father's riding master had never mentioned.

Captain Madrelar found him there, two sun-hands later. "So this is where you are! I've been searching the camp, *squire*." The emphasis he put on "squire" would have sliced wood. "I need you in my quarters."

Luden scrambled to his feet, threw the rigging over his shoulder, put his arm through the bridle, and hitched his saddle onto his hip. The captain had turned away; Esker got up and tucked the trailing reins into the rigging on his shoulder. Luden nodded his thanks and followed the captain back to his tent.

There he endured a blistering scold for his venture out to pick berries and his interfering with the troopers at their tasks. Finally, the captain ran down and left the tent, with a last order to "Put that mess away, eat your dinner without saying a word, and be ready to ride in the morning."

Luden put his tack on the rack next to the captain's, shivering with reaction. He'd been scolded plenty of times, but always he'd understood what he'd done wrong. What was so bad about gathering food for others and learning more that soldiers needed to know? He hadn't been gossiping or gambling.

He looked around the tent for something useful to do. A scattering of maps, message tubes, and papers covered the table. He heard the clang of the dinner gong; he could clear the table before the cook's assistant brought the captain's meal. He'd done that before; the captain never minded.

Luden picked up the first papers then stopped, staring at a green and black seal, one he had seen before. Had the captain found it somewhere? It was wrong to read someone else's papers, but this was Immer's seal. The *enemy's* seal. The hairs rose on his scalp as he read. Captain Madrelar—the name leapt out at him—was to put his troop at the service of the Duke of Immer, by leading them into an ambush, four hundred of Immer's men, within a half-day's ride of the crossroads Madrelar had shown him. For this Madrelar would receive the promised reward and a command. If he had been able to talk Fallo into sending one of his nephews or grandsons along, then Madrelar should drug or bind the sprout and send him to Cortes Immer.

Luden dropped the paper as if it were on fire and started shaking. It was the most horrible thing he could imagine. The captain a traitor? Why? And what was *he* supposed to do? He was only a squire, and how many of these men outside, these hardened mercenaries, were also traitors?

He had not understood fear before. He had thought, those times he climbed high in a tree, or jumped from a wall, that the tightness in his belly was fear, easily overcome for the thrill with it. This was different—fear that hollowed out his mind and body as a spoon scoops out the center of a melon. His bones had gone to water. All he'd heard of Immer—the tortures, the magery, the way Andressat's son had been flayed alive—came to mind. As soon as the captain came back and saw that he'd moved things on the desk, he might be overpowered, bound, doomed.

He had to get away before then…somehow. Even as he thought that, and how impossible it would be, his hands went on working, shuffling several other messages on top of Immer's, squaring the sheets to a neat stack. He rolled the maps as he usually did, noting even in his haste the marks the captain had made on one of them. They were not two days' ride from the crossroads, but one: the captain had lied to him. He put the maps in the map-stand as always. What now? He glanced out the tent door. No immediate escape: the cook's assistant was almost at the tent with a basket of food, and the captain had already started the same way, talking to his sergeant.

Luden took the dinner basket from the cook and had the captain's supper laid out on the table by the time the captain arrived. When the captain came in, he stood by the table, hoping the captain could not detect his thundering heart. The captain stopped short.

"Who did this?"

"Sir, I laid out your dinner as usual."

"You touched my papers? When?"

"To have room for the dinner." Luden gestured at the stack of papers at the end of the table. "It took only a moment, to stack them and put the maps away. Just as usual."

"Hmph." The captain sat and pointed to his cup. "Wine. And water."

Luden poured, his hand shaking. The captain gave him a sharp look.

"What's this? Still shivering from a scold? I hope you don't fall off your mount with fright if we do meet the enemy." The captain stabbed a slab of meat, cut it, and put it in his mouth.

Madrelar said nothing more in the course of the meal, then ordered Luden to take the dishes back to the cook, and eat his own dinner there. "I will be working late tonight," he said. "It's dry; sleep outside, and don't be sitting up late with the men. They need their rest. We ride early."

Luden could not eat much, not even the berry-speckled dessert. What was the captain up to, besides betrayal? Were the other men, or some of them, also part of it? Was the captain really prepared to sacrifice his own troops? And why? Luden's background gave him no hint. He tried to think what he might do.

Could he run away? He might escape the sentries set around camp on foot, but the horse lines had a separate guard. He could not sneak away on horseback. And even if he did escape afoot, he might be captured before he reached home—they had ridden hard to get here, and going back would take him longer. Especially since he had no way to carry supplies.

What then could he do? He looked around for Esker, but didn't see him, and dared not wander around the camp, in case the captain looked for him. Finally, he went back to the captain's tent. A light inside cast shadows on the wall…two people at least were in it.

Outside, near the entrance, he found a folded blanket and a water bottle on top of it. The captain clearly meant for him to stay outside. He picked them up, went around the side of the tent, rolled himself in the blanket, and—sure he could not sleep—dozed off.

He woke from a dream so vivid he thought it was real, and heard his voice saying "Yes, my lord!" He lay a moment, wide awake, chilled by the night air. The dream lay bright as a picture in his mind: his great-uncle, the Duke of Fall, speaking to all the children as he did every Midwinter Feast. *It is not for wealth alone, or tradition, that the Dukes of Fall have ruled here for ages past, since first we came from the South. But because we keep faith with our people. Never forget what you owe to those who work our fields, who take up arms to defend us. They deserve the best we have to give them.* And then the phrase that had wakened him: *Luden, look to your honor.*

He was a child of Fallo; he was the only one of that House here, and these men around him—some of them at least, and maybe all but the captain—were being led to slaughter. He still had honor, and the duty that came with honor.

And he badly needed the jacks. He threw off his blanket and stood up. Overhead, stars burned bright in the clear mountain air; he could see the tips of the tallest mountains, snow at their peaks even in summer, pale against the night sky, and enough silvery light glimmered over the camp to show him the way.

He had taken but ten steps toward the jacks when someone grabbed his arm and swung him round.

"And where d'you think you're going?"

It was Sergeant Pastak. Had the captain set a watch over him? Of course: he would need to, just in case. And so the sergeant was in on it, also a traitor.

"To the jacks," Luden said, glad his voice sounded slightly annoyed.

"To be sure, the jacks," the sergeant said, with a sneer. "Young lads…always eager to go to war until they get closer to it. Thinking of that, are you?"

"I'm thinking I ate too many of those berries before I gave the rest to the cook," Luden said. "And I need the jacks."

The sergeant shook his arm; Luden stumbled. "Just know, lad, you're with a fighting troop, not some fancy-boy's personal guards. You're not running off home."

That was clear enough. He stiffened against the sergeant's arm and adopted a tone he'd heard from his elders. "I am not one to run away, Sergeant. But I would prefer not to mark my clothes with berry juice and have someone like you think it was fear."

The sergeant let go of his arm as if it had burned him. "Well," he said. "The young cock will crow, will he? We'll see how you crow when the time comes—if it does." He gestured, the starlight running down his mail shirt like molten silver. "Go on then. To the jacks with you, and if you mark your clothes red and not yellow, I'll call you worthy."

Red could mean blood and not berry juice. Luden held himself stiffly and stalked off to the jacks as if he hadn't thought of that. He was not the only one at the jacks trench, though he was glad to see he had room to himself. He did have a cramp, and what he had eaten the previous day, berries and all he was sure, came out in a rush. He waited a moment, two, and then, as he stood, saw another man nearby.

"All right, Luden?" It was Esker. "The berries were good, but

I think they woke me up."

"I ate handfuls raw," Luden said.

"That can do it. These mountain berries—they look like the ones back in the lowlands, but they clear the system, even cooked."

Could he trust Esker? He had to do something, and Esker was the only one he had really talked to. "Esker, I have to tell—"

"I thought I told you to leave the soldiers alone, sprout!" It was the captain. No doubt the sergeant had told him where Luden was. "No chatter. Get to your blanket and stay there. And no more berries on the morrow." Luden turned to go. Behind him, he heard the captain. "Well, Esker? Sucking up to the old man's brat?"

"He had the gripe, captain, same as me. You know those mountain berries. I'd have sent him back in a moment."

Then murmurs he could not hear. Back near the tent, a torch burned; the sergeant stood beside it. Luden returned to his blanket and lay down, feigning sleep. He knew they would not leave him unwatched. Once again, sleep overtook him.

He woke to a boot prodding his ribs. "Hurry up. It's almost daylight."

Stars had faded; the sky glowed, the deep blue called Esea's Cloak, and the camp stirred. Horses whinnied, men were talking, laughing, he smelled something cooking. As he rolled his blanket, the captain stood by, watching. Luden yanked the thongs snug around it, and stood with it on his shoulder.

"Don't forget your water," the captain said. "You'll be thirsty later."

Luden bent to pick up the water bottle.

"Your tack's over there." The captain pointed to a pile on the ground; two men were already taking down the captain's tent.

Luden picked up his tack and headed for the horse lines.

"If you've no stomach for breakfast," the captain said, "put some bread in your saddlebags; you'll want it later."

He saddled his mount, put the water bottle into one saddlebag and then carried the bags to the cook for bread. Troopers were taking a loaf each from a pile on a table.

"Captain thought you'd like this," the cook said, handing him a spiced roll. "Gave me the spice for it special, and said put plenty of honey in it."

Luden's stomach turned. "It'll be too sweet if it's all I have. Could I have some plain bread, as well?"

The cook grinned. "You're more grown up than that, you're saying? Not just a child, to eat all the sweets he can beg?" He handed Luden a small plain loaf from the pile. "There. Eat troops' rations if you'd rather, but don't tell the captain; he only thought to please you."

"Thank you," Luden said. The sweetened roll felt sticky. He put both rolls in the other saddlebag, and then went to the jacks trench a last time. It was busy now; Luden went to one end, squatted, fished in the saddlebag for the roll, sticky with honey, that he was sure had some drug in it. He dropped it in the trench, then stood and grabbed the shovel, and covered it quickly.

"That's not your job," one of the men said. "Go back to the captain, get your gear tied down tight. Here—give me the shovel."

"I'll see him safe," another said. Esker.

Luden glanced in the trench; no sign of the roll. Unless someone had seen him drop it…he looked at Esker. "Thank you," he said. All at once it occurred to him that the formality of the duke's house—the relentless schooling in manners, in what his great-uncle called propriety—had a use after all. Underneath, he was still frightened, but now he could play other parts.

"Come on, then," Esker said. When they were a short distance from the trench, Esker said, "There was something you wanted to tell me last night. Still want to tell me in daylight? Is it that you're scared?"

As a rabbit before the hounds he wanted to say, but he must not. Instead, in a rush, he said, "The captain's going to betray you all to Immer's men; four hundred are coming to meet us."

Esker caught hold of his shoulder and swung him around. "Boy. Fallo's kin. That cannot be true, and we do not like liars."

"I'm not lying," Luden said. "I saw it—"

"Or sneaking."

"—a message from Immer, with Immer's seal."

Esker chewed his lip a moment. "You're certain?"

"Immer's seal, yes."

"I am an idiot," Esker said, "if I believe a stripling lad when I have ridden with the captain these eight years and more." He stopped abruptly, then pulled Luden forward. In a low growl: "Do not argue. There's no time; I can do nothing now. If it's true I will do what I can." Luden saw the captain then, staring at them both. Esker raised his voice. "Here he is, captain. Lad had a hankering to fill a jacks trench; Trongar saw him. I'm bringing him back to you." He sounded cheerful and unconcerned.

"I saw you head to head like old friends," the captain said.

"That, captain, was me telling him the *second* time that he had years enough for filling jacks trenches and you'd be looking for him. He's just young, that's all."

"That he is," the captain said, looking down at Luden. "Did you saddle that horse?"

"Yes, sir," Luden said. "And I thank you for that sweet loaf the cook gave me. Cook said you told him to put spice in it as well as honey."

The captain smiled. "So I did. You can eat it midmorning, when we rest the horses, since I doubt you've eaten breakfast after last night's adventure with berries."

"That's so, sir," Luden said. "It still gripes a bit."

"Today will take care of that," the captain said. "Riding a trot's the best thing for griping belly." He turned to the trooper. "Very well, Esker, I have him under my eye now; get back to your own place."

"Yes, Captain," Esker said. "Not a bad lad, sir. Just eager to help."

"Too eager," the captain said, "can be as annoying as lazy."

"True. So my own granfer told me."

Both men laughed; Luden's heart sank. He did not think Esker was a traitor, but clearly the man thought him just a foolish boy.

They were mounted when the first rays of sunlight fired the treetops to either side. When they reached the North Trade Road, their shadows lay long and blue before them. To either side, the forest thickened to a green wall and rose up a hill on the north side. Luden couldn't see the mountains now, but he could feel the cool air sifting down through the trees, fragrant with pine and spruce. Here and there he saw more bushes covered with berries. The captain pointed out a particularly lush patch.

"Tempted to stop and pick some?"

"No, sir."

"Good. Wouldn't want your belly griping again." A moment later, "Ready for that sweet bread yet?"

"No, sir," Luden said. "It's not settled yet."

"Ah. Well, you'll eat it before it spoils, I daresay."

The sun was high, their shadows shorter, when a man on horseback leading a pair of mules loaded with packs came riding toward them. He wore what looked like merchants' garb, even to the soft blue cap that slouched to one side. But it was the horse Luden noticed. He knew that horse.

That bay stallion with a white snip, uneven front socks, and a shorter white sock on the near hind had been stolen—along with fifteen mares—from a Fallo pasture the year before. Before that, it had been one of the older chargers used to teach Luden and his cousins mounted battle skills. Luden knew that horse the way he would know his own shirt; he had brushed every inch of its hide, picked dirt out of those massive hooves. And so the man riding him must be Immer's agent.

"Sir," he said to the captain. "That man's a horse thief."

"Don't be ridiculous," the captain said.

"I know that horse," Luden said.

"The world is full of bays with three white feet," the captain said. "It's just a merchant. Perhaps he'll tell us if he's seen any sign of brigands or—unlikely—Immer's troops."

"I'm telling you, I know that horse!"

The captain turned on him, furious. "You know *nothing*. You are a mere child, foisted on me by your great-uncle, Tir alone knows why, and you will be quiet or I will knock you off that horse and you can walk home alone."

Luden clamped his jaw on what he wanted to say and stared at the merchant instead. For a merchant, he sat the stallion very much like a cavalry trooper, his feet level in the stirrups, his shoulders square…and what was a merchant doing with the glint of mail showing at his neck? What was that combination of straight lines under the man's cloak? Not a sword…

The stallion stood foursquare, neck arched, head vertical, ears pointed forward. Luden checked his memory of the markings. It had to be the same horse.

Luden glanced at the captain, who raised his arm to halt the troop, then rode forward alone. Now was his only chance. Would the horse remember the commands? He held out his hand, opened and closed his fist twice, and called. "Sarky! *Nemosh ti!*"

At the same moment, a bowstring thrummed; Luden heard the crossbow bolt thunk into the captain's body, saw the captain stiffen, then slide to one side, even as the bay stallion leapt forward, kicking out behind; its rider lurched, dropped the crossbow and grabbed at the saddle.

"*Ambush!*" Luden yelled, "Ambush—form up!" He drew his sword and spurred toward Sarky; the stallion landed in a series of bucks that dumped its rider on the ground. Its tack glinted in the sun; instead of saddlebags, a polished round shield hung from one side of the saddle, and a helmet from the other. Bolts hummed past Luden; he heard them hitting behind him and kept going. Horses squealed, men cursed. The captain now hung by one foot from a stirrup, one bolt in his neck, two more bolts in his body; he bled from the mouth, arms dragging as his horse shied this way and that.

Luden had no time wonder why the enemy had shot the captain who'd done what he was hired to do. A crossbow bolt hit his own mount in the neck, then another and another. It staggered and went down. Luden rolled clear as the horse thrashed, but stumbled on a stirrup getting to his feet and fell again. He looked around—the old bay stallion was close beside him, kicking out at the fallen rider who now had a sword out, trying to reach Luden.

"Sarky," he called. "*Vi arthrin dekost.*" In the old language, "Lifebringer, aid me."

The stallion pivoted on his forehand, giving Luden the

position he needed to jump, catch the saddlebow, and scramble into the saddle from the off side, still with sword in hand. The man on the ground, quick witted, grabbed the trailing reins and held off the stallion's lunge with the point of his sword.

"Here he is—Fallo's whelp—help me, some of you!"

Luden scrambled over the saddlebow, along the horse's neck, and sliced the bridle between the horse's ears. The stallion threw his head up; the bridle fell free. The man, off balance, staggered and fell backward. Luden slid back into the saddle just as the horse jumped forward, forefeet landing on the fallen man. He heard the snap and crunch of breaking bones.

Mounted soldiers wearing Immer's colors swarmed onto the road. Ganarrion's smaller troop was fully engaged, fighting hard—and he himself was surrounded, separated from them. He fended off the closest attackers as best he could, yanking his dagger from his belt, though he knew it might break against the heavier curved swords the enemy used. The horse pivoted, kicked, reared, giving him a moment to cut the strings of the round shield and get it on his arm.

He took a blow on the shield that drove his arm down, got it back up just in time, parried someone on the other side with his own blade, and with weight and leg aimed his mount in the right direction—toward the remaining Ganarrion troopers. The stallion, unhampered by bit or rein, bullied the other mounts out of his way—taking the ear off one, and biting the crest of another, a maneuver that almost unseated him. Arm's length by arm's length they forced their way through the enemy to rejoin the Ganarrion troop—itself proving no easy prey, despite losses of horses and men.

"Tir's guts, it's the squire!" someone yelled. "He's alive." A noise between a growl and a cheer answered him.

Luden found himself wedged between two of the troopers, then maneuvered into the middle of the group. He saw Esker; the man grinned at him then neatly shoved an enemy off his horse.

"We need to get out of here!" someone yelled.

"How? Which way? They're all over—!"

"Luden!" Esker shouted over the din. "WHERE?"

He saw other glances flicking to him and away as the fight raged. They were waiting—waiting for him to make a decision. *What* decision? He was only a squire, he couldn't—but he had to: he was Fallo here. "BACK!" he yelled. "Take word back—warn them! Follow me!"

He put his spurs to Sarky, forcing his way between the others to the east end of the group. Twice he fended off attacks, and once he pushed past a wounded trooper to run his sword into one of the enemy. When he reached the far end of the group, he yelled "Follow me!" again and charged ahead, into a line three deep of enemy riders. Sarky crashed into one of the horses; it slipped, fell, and opened a gap.

For a terrifying time that seemed to last forever, Luden found himself fending off swords, daggers, a short lance, hands grabbing for him, trying to keep himself and his mount alive. He felt blows on his back, his arms, his legs; he could not think but only fight, hitting as hard as he could anything—man or horse—that came close enough. The noise—he had never imagined such noise—the screaming of men and horses, the clash of swords. Someone grabbed his shield, tried to pull him off the saddle; he hacked at the man's wrist with his sword; blood spurted out as the man's hand dropped away.

Always, the stallion pushed on, biting and striking, and behind him now he heard the Ganarrion troopers. One last horseman stood in his way; he felt Sarky's sides swell, and the stallion let out a challenging scream; that rider's mount whirled and bolted.

"*Kerestra!*" Luden said. Home. Despite his wounds, the stallion surged into a gallop. Behind, more yells and screams and a thunder of hooves that shook the ground. Luden dared a glance back. Behind him were the red and gray surcoats of Ganarrion's troop—more than half of them—and behind them the green and black of Immer's. How far could they run, how far could Sarky run, with blood flowing from a gash on his shoulder, with thick curds of sweat on his neck?

Ganarrion's troops had the faster horses, and opened a lead, but Sarky slowed, laboring. Esker rode up beside Luden. "Only a little farther, and we can give your mount a rest. Were you wounded?"

"I don't think so," Luden said. "I was hit, but it doesn't hurt."

"We'll see when we stop. Where do we go from here?"

"Straight back to Fallo. Tell the first troops we see that Immer's on the way."

"I thank you for the warning," Esker said. "And more, for getting us out of that."

"It was mostly Sarky," Luden said. The stallion flicked an ear back at his name.

One of the troopers in the rear yelled something Luden did not understand; Esker did. "They've halted and turned away," he said. "They may come on later, but it's safe to slow now as soon as they're out of sight. But it's your command."

"Mine?" Luden looked at Esker.

"Of course, sir—young lord—I mean. Captain and sergeant are dead; you're the only person of rank. And you got us out of that."

"Then…can we slow down now?"

Esker looked ahead and behind. "I'd say up there, young lord, just over that rise. Shall I post a lookout there?"

"Yes," Luden said, wishing he'd thought of that. By the time they cleared the rise, the old stallion had slowed to an uneven trot. The troop surrounded them as the stallion stood, sides heaving.

"By all the gods, young lord, I thought we were done for!" said one of the men. "Esker told me what you said. I didn't believe it until it happened."

"Kellin, see to his horse. That's a nasty shoulder wound. Hrondar, we need a watch over the rise," Esker said.

Luden slid off the stallion; his legs almost gave way. The smell of blood, the sight of it on so many, men and horses both. Several of the men were already binding up wounds.

"You are bleeding," Esker said to him. "Here, let me see." He slit Luden's sleeve with his dagger, and there was a gash. Luden looked at it then looked away. "That needs a battle-surgeon," Esker said. "But we can stop the bleeding at least. Sit down. Yes, right down on the ground."

He called one of the other men over; for a few moments, Luden struggled to keep from making a noise. Now that he was sitting down, his arm throbbing, he felt other injuries. Esker looked him over, pronounced most of them minor, though two would need a surgeon's care, and offered a water bottle. Luden remembered that his was on the saddle of the horse that had fallen under him. Also that he'd had no breakfast and the loaf in his saddlebag was as distant and unobtainable as his own water bottle. Around him now, the troopers were eating.

"Here," Esker said, tearing off a piece of his own. "Eat this— too bad you lost the one the captain gave you—honey would be good for you about now."

"It was poisoned," Luden said. He bit off a hunk of roll.

"How do you know that?"

"The letter I saw, with Immer's seal. It wasn't just the ambush. He was also supposed to bring a member of Fall's family for them to take back to Cortes Immer."

"You—but he said you were a nuisance he had to bring along."

Luden shrugged. That hurt; he took another bite of bread. The longer he sat, the more he hurt, though bread and water cleared his head. He looked around. Kellin had smeared some greenish salve on Sarky's wounds. "Give me a hand," he said, reaching up.

Esker put a hand down, and Luden stood.

"How long do the horses need to rest?" Luden asked.

Esker stared at him a moment. "You don't want to camp here?"

"We don't know where they are. They could be circling round, out of our sight. We need to move—" He stopped. Sarky's head had come up, ears pricked toward the east. Other horses stared the same way.

"Tir's gut, we didn't need this," Esker said.

A shrill whistle from the west, from the lookout on the rise; Luden tensed. Esker grinned. "It's our folk," he said.

"Our folk?"

"Ganarrion." He leaned closer. "Your command, young lord, but we'd look better mounted and moving. Even slowly."

"I'll need a leg up," Luden said, then, "Mount up! We'll go to meet them." Esker helped him into the saddle; the others mounted, and the lookout in the rear trotted up to join them. Luden's head swam for a moment, but he nudged Sarky into a walk; the troop formed up behind him.

In moments, he could see the banner, larger than the one his own cohort carried: Ganarrion himself was with them. Behind Ganarrion's company came another, Count Vladi's black banner in the lead. Ganarrion rode directly to Luden.

"Boy! What happened? Where's Captain Madrelar?"

Luden stiffened at the tone. "Madrelar's dead. He led us into ambush."

"WHAT?" Ganarrion's bellow echoed off the nearest hill.

"We were led into ambush; the enemy shot Madrelar, and we're all that fought free."

Ganarrion sat his horse as if stunned, then turned to his own company. "Sergeant Daesk, scouts out all sides, expect enemy contact. Cargin, fetch the surgeon; we have wounded." Then, to Luden he said, "You're Luden Fall, is that right? Prosso's son?"

"Yes, sir," Luden said.

"The duke told me to look for you. And that horse—if I'm not mistaken, that's one of the duke's horses, stolen a while back. And, no bridle? How did you—or I suppose the troop surrounded you?"

"No, my lord," Esker said. "Lord Fall warned us of the ambush then led us out, fighting all the way."

Lord Fall? He was no lord; he was barely a squire.

"Barely a squire," Esker continued, echoing Luden's thought, "but he took command when Madrelar and Pastak died, and led the charge that broke us out."

"And it was treachery?"

"Yes."

Ganarrion chewed his mustache for a long moment, staring at Luden then nodded. "Thank you, Esker." He gave a short bow. "Lord Fall, with your permission, I will relieve you of command. You and your mount are both in need of a surgeon's care, and I have need of those of your troop who are still fit to fight. Will you release them to me?"

Luden bowed in his turn; his vision darkened as he pushed himself erect again. "Certainly, Lord Ganarrion. As you wish." Then the dark closed in.

* * *

He woke in a tent with lamps already lit. When he tried to move, he could scarcely shift one limb, and he hurt all over. The memory of Immer's letter came first, and for one terrifying moment he thought he lay bound, already on his way to the dungeons of Cortes Immer. Then he heard voices he knew—Sofi Ganarrion, Count Vladi, Esker. The events of the day reappeared in memory, hazy as if seen through smoke.

"It's unusual, certainly," Count Vladi was saying. "But I remember a certain young squire dancing with death when I was a captain in Kostandan...."

Ganarrion grunted. "I was young and foolish then."

"And brave and more capable than anyone expected. This lad was not foolish, for what other choices did he have? We shall have much to tell Duke Fall when we return."

* * *

Luden stood before the Duke of Fall, when he was again fit to ride and fight. Behind him were the men of Ganarrion's company; Sofi Ganarrion stood on his sword-side and his own father on his heart-side.

"Victory is sweet," the old man said, "but honor is bread and meat to the soul. Those who have both, even once in their lives, are fortunate beyond all riches. You *won* your spurs, Luden; I cannot give them to you. Let us say I found something of mine that I am too old to use, that might be of service to you."

He opened the box on the table between them and turned it around to show Luden. The spurs within were old, the straps burnished with wear. Luden's breath caught. The duke's own spurs? He didn't deserve—

"Men died, my lord," is what came out of his mouth before he could stop it. "Life was enough reward."

Duke Fall nodded. "You are right, nephew. And it is as much for your understanding as for your courage that these spurs are now yours. We will speak more later; for now, let your sponsors perform their duties."

His father and Sofi Ganarrion stepped forward, each taking a spur, then knelt beside him, fastening them to his boots.

The End

AUTHOR'S NOTE ON
MERCENARY'S HONOR

Whose honor is most at risk, and whose honor is most revealing of his potential? Ilanz Balentos, retired mercenary and aging ruler of a small fortified city, never planned to be captured by Aliam Halveric's red-headed squire. The wily old warrior persuades the squire to take him where he wants to go, to Aliam's camp, because he has a plan to make allies of Halveric Company and win a bloodless victory. Everyone behaves impeccably except, as usual, Cortes Vonja, but that's another story someday.

Publication note: "Mercenary's Honor" was originally published in *Operation Arcana*, Baen Books, ed. John Joseph Adams, 2015.

MERCENARY'S HONOR

Ilanz Balentos looked at the wall around Margay and nod-ded his approval. It wasn't the best city wall he'd ever seen, but it was a start, a good start for a town that had been under Von-ja's so-called protection for many years. The town's leading mer-chants smiled. A wall—a defensible wall—had been one of his requirements before he would commit to living here the rest of his life and protecting people as they should be protected.

"You will sign the contract?" asked Ser Unglent, head of the local council.

"I will. You have done well. What did the Vonja militia think of it?"

"They told us we could not have a wall and were going to make us tear it down. We gave them wine and when they slept the lads took their weapons and next day—"

"Did you kill them all?"

"Kill? No! But we showed them we were more than they, and held their weapons, and they went away."

Ilanz winced inside. Civilians. If they had killed Vonja's militia rather than shaming them, Vonja might have let them alone. "Vonja will send more—perhaps even another mercenary company."

"But you are here."

"Yes. And we will protect you." That was the bargain: Margay to become his domain, and his own home, and his troops—or some of them, the ones who would stay when there was no promise of plunder—would protect them. Margay independent, as it had been once, rather than paying taxes to a distant city that never bothered to care for it. "Did you find that wizard you spoke about last time?"

"No…we sent an envoy to Sorellin's fair, and he asked, but the wizard said we were too small and could not pay enough."

Bad news, but not too bad. Vonja never took wizards on campaign anyway. Ilanz could protect Margay without a wizard's tricks.

He signed the contract, stamped it with his seals—the seal of the Company he had commanded for thirty-one years, and the new seal he'd had made, naming him Count Margay. The merchants had already signed, and then there was handshaking and talk and food and drink until at last he could climb up the stairs to the bedroom in the house he had chosen.

The long plan had come to fruition. He gave a thought to the mercenaries Vonja had hired this year to do the work their own militia should be doing…protect farmers from brigands and incursions from neighboring lands, policing traffic on their sections of the Guild League trade roads. Halveric Company had been in Aarenis only five campaign seasons, but already had a good reputation. Ilanz had no doubt he and his could defeat Halveric, if it came to it, if the Council at Cortes Vonja sent them this way, but he hoped it would not come to that. He had met the young man in Valdaire several times and liked what he knew of him.

* * *

The wall was an arm's-length higher by the time Ilanz's scouts saw Halveric Company marching up the road from Pler Vonja. Ilanz wondered what Vonja had told him about Margay. Almost certainly not the whole truth, knowing Vonja's history.

The younger commander had sense: he stopped a prudent distance away and sent two scouts forward at night, both circling wide of the town. One was captured after he stumbled into a large bramble patch and made so much noise Ilanz's own militia could not resist "rescuing" him. They sent him back to his own camp. The other was seen only as a shadow in shadows, heading for the Sorellin border. Of course the young commander would want to know if Sorellin backed Margay. Perhaps his men would catch this one on the way back.

Perhaps he could send a message to young Halveric that way. If they come to battle, it would be a bloody business, killing a lot of good mercenaries for the profit of Vonja in the Guild League...and maybe that was what Vonja planned. Some realms hated and feared mercenaries, even if they hired them. If that was Vonja's plan, weakening or destroying two competent mercenary companies—then not only Halveric but other companies were at risk. He paced his office, on the second level of his new house, thinking out the possibilities, and finally sat down to write a message. He would send it even if his people didn't catch that scout. For the rest of the day, he went out in the town, chatting with his citizens and his own soldiers. At dinner, he told his captains his plan to attempt a truce with Halveric.

"I'm not sure, Commander...my lord, I mean."

Ilanz waved his hand. "Never mind formalities. This is a military conversation. What's your assessment of young Halveric?"

"Smart, tough, increasingly competent, and...a very solid

sense of honor. I cannot see him breaking a contract, even with Vonja."

"He has presented himself as a man of honor, that is true," Ilanz said. "But there is more than one kind of honor. If, as I suspect, Vonja has lied to him, has broken faith with him, I think—I hope—he will see that keeping faith with the faithless is foolish, and merely teaches our employers that they can break their word to us with impunity." He spread his hands on the table, the scarred hard hands of a man thirty years a mercenary. One finger missed a joint, two had healed crookedly from being broken. "If he does not, we will have to fight him, and that will cost us. And him. And possibly the town as well, not only from the losses to our force, but...well...nothing in war is known until the battle's over."

Finally, late that night, he went to bed, leaving the single lamp burning as always. He had to know, the instant he awoke, if he still had sight in one eye or had gone completely blind. He set his town shoes by the table, his boots at the end of the bed, his sword in the fold of blanket. Then he slept.

* * *

He woke face-down in his bed, a weight on his back and his wrists already bound. Whoever was there breathed heavily, had sweaty hands and a very sharp knee, and smelled of blood and unwashed male. He tried to twist his wrists free, and the weight shifted. A dagger tip lay under his right ear, just firm enough to make it unmistakable.

"Be quiet."

He nodded. By the feel, the bindings on his wrist were no thicker than shoe-laces. He could break those later, when the dagger was not so near his life. Weight left his back as whoever it was climbed off the bed, but the dagger's touch never left his neck. Someone with experience, then. A thief in his town? He was incensed; even a thief should recognize that Ilanz was the town's only hope of freedom.

"Who are you?" the voice demanded. "Tell me true. Will they ransom you?"

Ransom? What was this?

"Sit up!" the voice went on. "I want to see your face." A hand grabbed his shoulder, tugged. Ilanz rolled with the tug, giving momentary thought to the attack he could make as he rolled over and up to sitting, but the first glimpse of his assailant put that out of mind. He saw a stripling boy, his face disfigured by a rapidly swelling bruise from brow to cheekbone on the right side, but on the left—he knew that face, though the boy's sweat-darkened hair looked more brown than red in the lamplight.

"You're Halveric's squire," he said, keeping his voice low. "The redhead."

"You're Commander Balentos," the lad said. "I saw you in Valdaire."

Ilanz sent a quick prayer of thanks to Simyits; the trickster god had favored him once again. He could see now that the squire had one sleeve of a peasant shirt half-torn off, and blood marked it.

"Did you come to kill me?" he asked. If Halveric had sent an assassin, he had misjudged Halveric's character and would have to change his plans.

"No!" That sounded genuine, disgust and anger mixed. "I didn't know you were here until I...well, I was running away from them."

From Ilanz's own troops, presumably. "Why did you come into town?"

"They made me. I had to get away—"

"Well…what are you going to do now?"

He could practically see the thoughts running through the boy's head, the kind of thoughts any young squire would have. The boy had found and disabled the enemy commander…which in some circumstances would make him a hero…or dead. Glory, danger, fear, pride. What next? Would he think to kill Ilanz, threaten him and demand his own freedom, or—

"I will take you to my commander," the boy said.

Of course. Ilanz almost grinned; instead he nodded, keeping his expression serious. "That is a sensible thing to do."

"Sir—I mean—"

"Your commander needs to know what he faces here. I am the best person to tell him. You think clearly, young man. What is your name?"

A moment of silence; the boy started to scowl, then winced at the pain. How bad was that injury? Would the boy lose that eye? Then he answered. "Kieri Phelan…sir."

Mannerly, intelligent…Halveric must be a good teacher, as well as a good commander. And the boy himself was far out of the ordinary. High-born, almost certainly, and possessed of something very like the magery that cropped up now and again in Ilanz's own family.

"We cannot just go down and out the front, Kieri," Ilanz said. "My soldiers are too many for you to hold me at hazard if they see you. They would kill you to free me. How did you get in? Can we get out that way?"

"I…think so. Yes."

"Good. We should start. Only…I need something on my feet. I cannot walk to your camp barefoot." He looked at the floor beneath the table…there were his shoes, and sure enough the laces were missing. "Let me stick my feet in those—"

"You won't try to escape?"

Ilanz managed a shrug. "I have been wondering how to contact your commander. And here you are, offering to lead me. Although, as part of your education as squire, Kieri, you should not trust me. I might, after all, turn on you, grab that dagger, tie your hands, and march you straight up to your commander, which would be a disgrace, would it not?"

The boy's mouth quirked. "It would...and I do not intend to let that happen. There's a sword in your bed; I felt it when I climbed on—"

Inlanz shook his head. "Advice, and I swear by Tir it's true: do not take my sword. It is much easier to disarm a man with a sword than a man with a dagger, if you have my experience. Everything in this room is a weapon to me, were I free. Also—just to show my honesty in this—if I should stumble, do not out of pity unbind my hands. There is no one in all Aarenis who could govern my movements were I unbound." He watched the boy's face, saw comprehension as quick as he'd hoped. "Of course, that means you will have to help me put on those shoes." He stuck out one foot, and waited.

Another pause he did not quite understand, then the boy knelt, keeping his gaze on Ilanz's face, and picked up both shoes. Far more deftly than Ilanz expected, he slipped one shoe on the foot, then—as Ilanz put that foot down and lifted the other—put the other shoe on the other foot. For a wonder, he had them on the correct feet. Not everyone wore such shoes, but Ilanz had a bony growth on one foot that made them necessary.

"May I stand?" Ilanz asked.

"Make no rash moves," the boy said. "Over there, where a panel is open, stairs go down. Quietly..."

* * *

The night air was more chill than Ilanz expected and somewhere in the walk to Halveric's camp he got a small sharp stone in his left shoe. Simyits' price for the help earlier, he supposed. He'd paid more, in the past. Halveric's sentries were alert; he approved the way they reacted to the discovery of an enemy commander, barelegged in a nightshirt, being guided and guarded by a boy. No smirks, no laughter, but an escort to Halveric's tent.

Halveric was awake by the time they got there, boots on his feet and his shirt at least partly tucked into his trousers. Ilanz saw Halveric's eyes widen as he recognized Ilanz. Ilanz inclined his head.

"Commander Halveric," he said.

"Commander Balentos. I am...surprised."

"So would I be. Of your courtesy, if I give my pledge, could your men unbind my hands? I am, as you see, without weapons. And there is a stone in my left shoe."

"Donag," Halveric said. "Free Commander Balentos."

Ilanz stood still as two other soldiers stepped forward, swords out, and one moved behind him. He felt the cold edge of a dagger slide between his wrists and the thongs that bound them.

Halveric spoke to someone inside the tent. "Garris?"

A boy's voice answered. "Yes, m'lord?"

"Light us a lamp in the tent, and set up another chair."

Ilanz's hands fell free; he rubbed his wrists. Halveric's soldier put the cut pieces of shoelace in his hands and saluted, an unexpected courtesy. Halveric, he saw, had looked past him to his captor.

"Kieri, I am sure you have a report to give, but see the surgeon first, clean up, and dress."

"It's not my blood, m'lord," the boy said. "Or most of it isn't."

"That was an order, Squire." The boy bowed and left them. Then, to Ilanz, "He wasn't supposed to go into the town after you—he was supposed to go around the town to the border and find out if Sorellin troops were waiting to move in. Please—come into my tent and take some refreshment." He pulled the tent flap aside.

"He told me how he came to be sitting on my back tying my wrists," Ilanz said, limping forward. "I do not blame you; I did not think you were the sort to send an assassin. As it is, I am glad to have a chance to talk to you; there's a letter to you on my desk back there, which I had meant to send you tomorrow."

Halveric's tent was the size Ilanz's captains used—just one large room, with two cots on either side and room for a table and chairs in the middle. Ilanz sat down on one chair and kicked off his left shoe; the stone fell out. He looked at his foot—no blood, just a sore spot—and put the shoe back on.

Halveric poured wine and then water into two mugs and nodded to Ilanz. Ilanz picked up one; Halveric took the other, and they both sipped. "Would you like a robe?" Halveric asked.

Ilanz laughed. "Would I like a robe? I tell you, Commander Halveric, what I would like. I would like to be asleep in my own bed, wake up tomorrow after a full night's sleep, send you my letter, and hear in return that you agreed there was no profit in an assault on my town. That is what I would like."

Halveric looked back at him. "I have a contract," he said.

"Yes, of course you do. You contracted with Vonja—everyone in Valdaire knew they had come to you, and I would almost lay odds—though Simyits has been generous to me already tonight—that I know what they offered and what you argued them up to. I suspect they called you in when their troops came home empty-handed and offered you a bonus to put down a rebellion up here in Margay."

"They did." Halveric nodded. "But they did not tell me you were here. I had suspected your presence, and while we are being so open, I know you have more troops, and archers, than you had last year."

Ilanz chuckled. "I knew you were good. A squire like that red-haired lad is more useful picking information out of gossip than a trained spy, isn't he?"

"Several of them are," Halveric said. He got up and pulled a box out from under a cot with the covers all in a jumble. His, no doubt. While he rummaged inside, Balentos looked at the others: one squire snoring, a much younger one sitting up bright-eyed and curious on the most distant cot. The tent was orderly, but spare. Halveric had, he suspected, poured every nata of profit into his men's equipment and supplies. A good way to start, but now he should be learning to show his status.

The robe Halveric brought was broad enough—Halveric was his match in shoulders and chest—but short. Still, he looked and felt less like a beggar and more like a guest with it on.

"So," Halveric said, when he sat down again, dropping two long leather thongs on the table in front of Ilanz. "What was in your letter?"

Ilanz picked up a thong and threaded it through the slits in one shoe. "I will be brief. Years ago, when I myself held a contract with Vonja, I was sent up here to deal with a border issue with Sorellin, and first saw Margay. Just such a place, I thought, as I would like to retire in, but very badly governed. They saw the tax collectors and the militia escorting them twice in the year, but no help whatever with Sorellin incursions or brigands down from the mountains." He picked up the other thong and refastened his other shoe.

Halveric nodded but said nothing.

"So a few campaign seasons ago, when I heard rumors of the town considering rebellion, I made a short visit. By myself. They remembered me; I had occasionally visited before. I talked to their town council, and we came to an agreement. The protection I could give, in trade for their allegiance to me as a lord. I advised them on fortifications—how to build new houses, how to arrange the town a little differently, how to build a wall. We set up regular courier contact."

"You...encouraged them to rebel?"

"They were going to anyway. And in this location they would be constantly harassed by Vonja and Sorellin squabbling over them. You know where that leads."

"Yes," Halveric said. "Destruction, ruined crops, dead civilians."

"I can prevent that," Ilanz said. He straightened, easing his back. "Maybe even long enough for it to last, though I can't promise. Didn't promise. And I will tell you what I think, from your expression, you have already seen in the light of this lamp: I am going blind. One eye already—and all the gold I spent for wizards' potions and spells and the prayers of every priest who would listen only slowed the blindness. They tell me the other eye will go as well, and cannot tell me how long—a few years, perhaps ten. That's why I decided on this, a place I could stay and defend. I don't need two good eyes for that. So—you said Vonja lied to you about the situation up here?"

"Greedy merchants who didn't want to pay taxes, maybe gulled by Sorellin which has sought to encroach before. Small town, hardly more than a village, just a waystation on the north trade route, no war experience, no fortifications, should be simple." Halveric said that in a mincing falsetto. Then he grinned, showing teeth. "I don't believe it when someone says it will be simple."

"Mmm. Have you seen Margay since your own last visit—four years ago, wasn't it?"

"No."

"We now have a wall well over man-high, with appropriate reinforcement at the gates. Streets redesigned for defense, with some fortified buildings. Ample stores and water to withstand a siege...and my troops."

Halveric uttered something in a foreign tongue that crackled with anger.

Ilanz didn't need to know the words; he knew the tone. "You run a good company, Commander Halveric," he said. "I do not think it is as good as mine—that comes with more experience—but on some days you might defeat us. A battle between us could be—would be—ruinous for us both." He paused. Would Halveric get the point? Would he say it if he did?

"You think Vonja wants us to destroy each other?"

"I wish I knew Sorellin's role in this," Ilanz said, stretching his legs. "Do they want Margay for themselves? They did once. Or do they agree with Vonja that there's a danger of mercenaries becoming too powerful?"

"Their envoy said they had no interest in Margay, but refused to say Sorellin would not let Margay in if it won free of Vonja."

"They still want it, then. And if Margay is weakened enough by a battle between your people and mine, they may come and take it."

Halveric sat forward. "Look here...it's clear you want me to break my contract and just go away—"

Ilanz shook his head. "No. You are smart enough to know Vonja will have spies out in the hills—Sorellin will too. I think you should proceed as you would have, up to a point: send out scouts, discover that the town is heavily fortified and defended, and—what would you do then?"

Halveric shrugged. "My contract requires me to try to take it, reduce the rebellion, and bring the guilty parties to Pler Vonja."

"Yes. And if they had told you the truth about what you faced up here, would you have accepted the additional assignment?"

"I….probably not. We've never fought you, but we've heard from those who have…. You need a twenty percent advantage to win and fifty percent to win cleanly. And that's at the size you were before you hired more men last winter."

"So Vonja's lies put you in a situation where you must either break a contract—risking your reputation—or fight a battle against a superior force—risking not just lives but your Company's existence. Because you know, as well as I, how many you would lose in a direct confrontation. Do you know what Guild League law says about parties to a contract?"

"Does it say if one lies about its part the other can wiggle out of an obligation?" Halveric's jaw muscles bunched.

"More than that. The party misrepresenting serious danger may be brought before the Guild League's High Court and may be judged fraudulent, penalized with high fines, some portion of which comes back to the injured party. At least, I would think, the amount of your bonus and the unpaid part of your base contract." Ilanz took another swallow of the watered wine. Halveric's face had gone blank, his eyes mostly hidden beneath lowered lids. "And yes, a mercenary company has brought such an issue before the High Court and won. It doesn't make friends of the employer, but it does make the point that we are not mere sword-wheat, to be scythed down for profit." Another swallow, another glance at Halveric's face. The eyes were open now, watching him, the expression wary. "I know a judicar in Valdaire familiar with the law involved."

"You did that?"

"I was much younger and very, very angry. I lost a cohort of good men. So whatever Vonja really meant by this—was it just laziness and cowardice, or actual malice?—you should be aware of the legal situation."

"I have never broken a contract." Pride in that, but pride overlaying anger. No man could be happy with employers who lied to him, who knew a danger and did not reveal it.

"That is a good thing," Ilanz said. "A very good thing, but—" He raised a finger. "But you have another contract, do you not, with your men? And if you have a conflict of contracts, the one no commander should ever break is the one with his men. You are their only safety, their only hope. They depend on you in a way no employer does. You stand between them and an employer who would abuse them."

Halveric said nothing, staring at him, or through him; it was hard to see in the lamplight. All at once Ilanz felt old, exhausted. He felt the soreness where the stone had been; his back hurt; his eyes burned. Halveric was young and had his pride, a young man's pride; perhaps he himself had pushed too hard. His stomach rumbled suddenly, loud enough to be heard, and Halveric glanced at it, then back at Ilanz's face.

"I am sorry," he said. "My hospitality failed—and I am hungry, when I wake this time of night. I will send for food." Halveric's voice was gentle, courteous, but carried no other meaning, agreement or disagreement. Before Ilanz could think what to say, Halveric was already standing, moving to the tent door, speaking softly to the man outside. When he came back to the table, Halveric spoke to the boy still sitting on his cot. "Go to sleep,

Garris. Tomorrow will be busy." The boy scrambled back under his covers and rolled over.

"It won't be much, this time of night," Halveric said, in the same easy tone. "But we will both be better for some ballast to the wine, watered as it was."

"Your squire who brought me—Kieri, he said his name was—is that your son?" The boy looked nothing like Halveric, but perhaps the mother was very light. Ilanz wondered if she had also been a mage, or even perhaps an elf.

"No."

"He is...unusual. Remarkable, I would say, for a boy his age. There is power in him. He will be a fine commander some day, I judge, if he does not have a domain to take over when he inherits."

Halveric's expression sharpened. "Why do you say that?"

"What he said to me—how he was captured, how he escaped, and then how quickly he took advantage when he found himself in a room with a strange man asleep. From the way he carries himself, I would think his father a rich man, possibly even a king."

For a moment Halveric said nothing, then: "No, alas. If he... if he had an inheritance, it was lost to him. He came to us—to my home in the north—as a waif, homeless and hungry."

"Even more remarkable, then. You have done very well, to take such a one and turn him into this. May you have many sons, for you deserve them."

Even in lamplight, he could see a flush rise on Halveric's cheeks. "I did no more than any man would."

"My lord, here is food—" Kieri entered with a tray piled with raggedly-cut bread and pots Ilanz hoped contained honey or jam or even pan drippings.

"What did the surgeon say, Kieri?" Halveric asked, as the boy put the tray on the table and stood back.

"I am fine," the boy said. When Ilanz looked at his face, his eye had swollen completely shut now, and the bruise on that side of his face had darkened more. "I am not to get hit in the face again for four hands of days, he said."

Halveric handed a slice of bread drizzled with honey to Ilanz and another to the boy. "Here, Kieri—you must be hungry. Eat this and lie down, get some rest."

The boy took his slice of bread to his cot and ate. Ilanz bit into his slice and had finished that and another one before Halveric spoke again. The food settled his stomach and cleared his head.

"It is getting toward dawn," Halveric said first. "Cooks will be starting breakfast—there'll be more than just bread and honey then." He finished his own slice of bread, took a swallow of the watered wine, cleared his throat. "I...understand what you said. And I am trying to think clearly. And admitting to myself that you are my elder who—assuming you to be honest, and I have no reason to think you are not—knows more of Aarenis and war than I do, young as I am. About honor—yes, my people deserve my care absolutely. And yes, Vonja lied to me. But the contract— it is not a matter of law only, you see. I must feel that my gods agree."

Ilanz nodded. "I understand. That is exactly what a man of honor must do. I do not know what gods you follow..."

"I am Falkian. Do you know of Falk?"

"Indeed—the story is well-known in Aarenis. He served in place of his brothers, and they repaid that sacrifice with scorn."

"Yes. And so keeping a promise means a great deal to Falkians. To break one for any reason is a serious matter." A pause

Ilanz did not dare to break. Then Halveric sighed. "And yet I believe that you have the right of it, that my duty to my people is far greater than my duty to Vonja who lied to me. So tell me what it is you were thinking of—though I admit I am not happy if that means us turning tail and running away."

"It is not that," Ilanz said. "Here is what we might do instead."

*　*　*

Ilanz rode up to the gates of Margay on one of the captains' horses, wearing clothes borrowed from one of Halveric's soldiers and his own shoes with new laces. The guards at the gate gaped and wanted to ask questions.

"I haven't time," Ilanz said. "I've been to parlay with Halveric, and there's much to do. Send someone to fetch the captains; meeting in my office in half a sun-hand."

Halveric would be meeting with his captains by now, he was sure. He wished he could have stayed for that, but he was needed here. Already people were on the street, startled to see him riding an unfamiliar horse, wearing unfamiliar clothes. He smiled at them, greeted the ones he knew, but did not stop.

At the door of his own house stood a cluster of people with worried faces; they turned at the sound of hooves. "Sir—my lord—where you been?" Kemin, retired sergeant and now his servant, sounded half frightened and half angry.

"Preventing disaster, I hope," Ilanz said. He dismounted. "This fellow needs a bait of grain and a rub-down. I need breakfast, a bath, and my own clothes—I have a captains' meeting very shortly."

Someone came to take the horse; Kemin followed him into the house and upstairs. "Sir, please—"

"I had a busy night," Ilanz said. "But I'm here now, and you're welcome to sit in on the captains' meeting. Right now—a bath."

Bathed, dressed again, a platter of stirred eggs and ham consumed, he went down to his office and met the worried gaze of his captains. Before they could speak, he held up his hand. "We have a rare opportunity," he said. "And we must prepare at once. Halveric Company's commander has agreed to my proposal."

"They're leaving?"

"Not immediately." Ilanz outlined the situation—Vonja's lies, Halveric's contract, the certain presence of Vonjan spies—and his own solution.

"A mock battle?" Meltarin, his senior captain, scowled. "You trust them to hold to the bargain? Halveric hasn't broken a contract yet, and they're a good company."

"He has more reason to distrust me, than I to distrust him. And he took my point about his honor being tied to his men as well as to his employer. Now—here's the plan." Ilanz outlined it quickly; his experienced captains understood at once, and he released them to complete their parts of it, then instructed his majordomo to block up the entrance Kieri had used, posted two guards outside his bedroom, and went back to sleep for a few hours.

* * *

By the morning of the battle, two Vonja and two Sorellin spies had been caught and isolated in the town, high enough in the other tower house to see beyond the wall, but with only one small slit window to look out of. Ilanz had inspected the view from that window. It would have been easier to fake a battle if he'd been able to hire a wizard, but a narrow window high up would do. The local rag-picker had been paid for his entire stock of old clothes and ripped blankets; the local farmers had moved their flocks away from the designated field of battle, and the local butchers, though puzzled, contributed offal, skins, and jugs of blood.

Ilanz woke well before dawn, dressed and armed himself, and came down to find his men all in place, having eaten a battle meal just after the turn of night, as usual. He ate his own breakfast, then—as the sun rose through layers of mist—climbed to the top of the wall. Yes. There was Halveric Company's vanguard, exactly as agreed. Someone on a gray horse—Halveric himself, he thought—rode along the line.

Ilanz grinned, then walked along his own defenses, reminding his men to keep their swords scabbarded unless he himself gave the order to draw them or they were attacked with bare steel. They grinned back at him. Then he spoke to his council, reminding them that everyone but troops must stay indoors. "Do not mind the noise," he said. "There will be yelling and screaming and other noises. If they get so far, there may be pounding at the gates. Do not worry. I know all that is happening, and you will be safe."

They nodded, not looking particularly confident except for a group of young men who had staves in hand and had been—he knew—part of the group that had sent the Vonja militia home weaponless. "I'm sorry," Ilanz said now to that group. "You also must stay out of this. These are hardened soldiers come against us, not the Vonja militia. We will defeat them, but you are not, forgive me, a match for them. Later, you may join the militia here. Go home and protect your own houses from within."

Halveric's vanguard advanced, then halted suddenly, as if noticing the town's fortifications for the first time. Four men on horseback rode closer, halting outside bow range and peering at the wall, hands up to shield their eyes from the sun. Three rode away from the one on the gray horse, parallel to the wall around the town, then rode back to report. Arms waved. Hands pointed. It was, Ilanz thought, a masterful job of acting out disagreement in command and the senior commander's power to settle it.

He noticed also that Halveric had figured out which wooded rise Ilanz had placed several tens of archers on, and avoided giving them a close, easy flanking shot. Good thinking…but he had not anticipated the second trap. Ilanz's half-cohort of mounted archers swept in on Halveric's vanguard from the sun-side, and in seconds the battle was truly joined; instantly the morning quiet shattered into the sounds of battle: screams, bellows, horses' whinnying, hoofbeats, the thud of weapons on weapons and bodies. Flocks of birds burst from every tree and bush, adding to the confusion.

Halveric responded with an instant half-turn, facing three ranks of the vanguard cohort into the sun…excellent training and practice, Ilanz thought, and glanced up at the prisoners' window. They would see only part of that, which was exactly what he wanted. And then Halveric's surprise took his own in the flank—up from the tall grass sprang Halveric's own archers. Riders fell, infantry fell, and Halveric Company marched on, nearer, fending off the flank attack. The noise grew louder, the familiar sounds he had known so long. So far it seemed both sides fought with blunted weapons, not bare steel, but the prisoners should not be able to tell that at this distance.

Another cohort came into view. Ilanz signaled his nearest captain, lowered his own helm, and nudged his mount—Halveric's captain's mount—forward. His senior captain would lead the other half of those in town out the gate on the other side of town, supposedly out of Halveric's sight, though he knew the gate was there. Would he think of it?

Along with Ilanz's troops came both two-wheeled handcarts and wagons bearing his physicians and their gear, spare weapons, and the rags and offal and sheepskins and pots of blood he had ordered collected, all positioned on the far side of the troops from the prisoners' window.

As the sun climbed up the sky, the battle raged, noise and confusion, dust and smoke. At times the two armies pulled back, and water carriers ran up and down the ranks. Scattered bodies lay in the grass, some moving feebly and others motionless. Overhead, scavengers appeared, wheeling high over the battlefield, then swooping low to check out any unmoving body. A few even landed to start pecking.

Cohorts and parts of cohorts maneuvered, struggling for advantage, but as midday passed, it was clear that Halveric could not advance all the way to the walls, and had, indeed, been pushed back half the width of the big pasture. In midafternoon, they began a disciplined withdrawal; Ilanz's forces made short dashes at them, but did not press the pursuit. It looked as though the Halverics had lost almost a third of their force, leaving the brown-clad troops in command of the field, and well before dusk the Halverics had returned to the previous night's camp, helping their wounded. War-crows and vultures descended on the motionless figures. A half-glass later, Halveric appeared again, with a red flag, and Ilanz met him mid-field. He was glad to see that Halveric looked as dirty and tired as he himself felt. Practice or not, it had been a long, hard fight.

"A good training exercise," Ilanz said. "I had good reports of your company before, and now I know those were not exaggerated."

Halveric nodded. "I learned from you. You nearly took us at the start—I knew you had archers, but not mounted ones.

Where did you hide the horses last night?"

"Two hills back." Ilanz pointed. "But your counter-flanking movement was excellent. I knew you had anticipated my archery contingent in the woods—"

"May I just ask how many extra troops you got last winter? Were we really outnumbered, or are yours that much better?"

Ilanz laughed. "You were outnumbered. I hired fifteen tens, sent ahead in small groups, over the winter. No shame to you for needing to withdraw."

"Well, that's good to know." Halveric grinned back. "I thought we could hold longer than we did at evens."

"How much damage?" Ilanz asked. "We had some broken bones and a lot of bruises—outnumbered or not, your troops fight very well."

"Much the same, but for one death. Hit square in the throat on a backswing—choked—"

"That's bad...did you get him back?"

"Yes. Carried as wounded."

"Good. We can let the scavengers do their worst, then. Will you come to supper tonight?"

"Tomorrow, I think. Frankly, all I want now is a bath and a good sleep."

"I, also. Tomorrow, then."

* * *

The Captains' Banquet had been a great success; Halveric's captains and his own had exchanged names and stories, congratulated one another on the performance of their cohorts, and at a nod from Halveric, had excused themselves to go back to the camp, picking up any stray Halverics along the way. The prisoners would not be able to see any of the festivities.

Now Halveric and Ilanz had the terrace to themselves as the long summer twilight lingered and a fresh scent of green leaves and fruit came from the lower end of the house's walled garden. Ilanz sent thanks to Simyits and Tir, that they dined as friends, that only one had died in the training exercise. And thanks also that he would have, for the rest of his life, a place of his own. No more need to spent half a year in a tent, the rest in rented lodgings. When his sight failed, he would have this place, where he would know every wall, every door…and a sweet-scented garden. He drew a deep breath and let it out slowly.

He felt gratitude to Aliam Halveric as well, and hoped the younger man would accept a little more advice. Two things, in particular. He glanced over. Aliam, as he now called him, leaned back in his chair, legs stretched out before him. He looked like someone contemplating both success and a new worry.

"If I may," Ilanz began.

Aliam gave him a lazy smile. "If you're going to offer me more advice, Ilanz, go ahead. Your advice has been to my advantage so far."

"Well, then. You need a new tent, a tent fit for the commander you are, and will become: in your own colors, at least three rooms, and the front one kept for the reception of visitors. Table or two, chairs, your weapons on display, space to store maps and so on."

"I thought you were looking down your nose at my tent."

"No—I understood you spent first on your men and their needs, and that is good. So did I, when I began. But to deal with merchants who care more for gold than anything else, you must make a show."

Aliam nodded. "I take your advice, and as soon as I can, I'll order such a tent."

"And...one other thing."

"Yes?"

"In Valdaire, I have four more years' winter lease—Evener to Evener—of a caravanserai large enough for your company. I know you asked about it. But now, I will not need it. If you still want it, I will give you a note to the owner's factor: you can take over the lease." Aliam opened his mouth and Ilanz shook his head before Aliam could speak. "I want nothing back for it. By the gods, man, you could have killed me and did not. You kept to our bargain about the battle. You have acted, dare I say it, like the son I wish I had had, but never sired. And so, in this one thing, being a mercenary commander, I see myself your father, and give you what I would give a son."

To his surprise, Aliam's eyes glistened, as if tears were near. "Thank you, Ilanz," he said. "I am honored to be able to accept."

Ilanz thought of telling him more, but reflected that every man had his limits, where advice and gifts were concerned, and it was best to let the young learn for themselves.

The End

Author's Note on Consequences

Kieri Phelan, more than a decade older than in "Mercenary's Honor," has formed his own mercenary group, and gained—with great effort (and some hidden assistance)—his first independent contract. He is military advisor to the Crown Prince of Tsaia, and his single cohort of one hundred is the smallest in the army the Prince assembled to fight Pargunese invaders. Kirgan Marrakai, Duke Marrakai's eldest son, one of a group of young men traveling with their noble fathers to observe the battle, but too young to fight, takes exception to this mere mercenary advising the Prince. The full working out of consequences is beyond the scope of this story.

Publication note: An early draft of "Consequences" was published online at *Paksworld Blog*, serialized, 11/14/2022 to 11/24/2022.

CONSEQUENCES

One bright spring morning, the Tsaian army, commanded by the Crown Prince, marched north out of Vérella, between cheering crowds waving leafy branches and throwing flowers. Pargun had crossed their eastern border in winter; now this army would push the Pargunese back and be home victorious by midsummer. Every unit, from the Tsaian Royal Guard, in its rose-and-white uniforms, headed by the Crown Prince in his shining armor, his standard-bearers with the royal banner, to the feudal troops in the colors of their local lord, including the Girdish militias in blue and gray under their Marshal, was led by a mounted commander, many splendid in shining armor with ribbons or plumes at the peaks of their helmets.

All but one. One small group, one hundred and one strong, infantry with short swords and shields, marched under the pennant of no land-holder at all but a foreign mercenary captain. They wore maroon uniforms, scantly trimmed in white, simple helmets, and carried what looked like leather packs on their backs. On their single banner, maroon bordered a white central bar on which a maroon fox mask smirked out at the world.

Its commander marched with his men, on foot, through the city. His helmet bore no ribbons or plume. It concealed his hair, but his fox-red beard suggested its color. He had armor—breast and back, forearms, shin-guards over his boots—and his sword was longer than his men's. On his heart-side, what must be his sergeant walked a step behind him. They all—including the captain—looked not just fit but hard, dangerous. Troops that had fought more than the locals had ever drilled. The crowd did not cheer them; a small bubble of silence kept pace with them, after the first excited shouts for the Prince and Royal Guard. Cheers began again when the next unit passed.

Beyond the city, beyond the last pavement, as the head of the column turned east on a farm lane between an orchard and a field, the lead horses of the Royal Guard and the team pulling the Crown Prince's personal wagon raised dust that soon rose to a towering cloud. Past the farms lay open grassland and scattered woods.

Mounted leaders strayed to windward, mostly out of the dust, but the captain of that small contingent soon looked as dusty as his troop. His clothes, maroon with white trim, like his troops, turned gray with it. His face was masked in dust, his fox-red beard dulled with it. His armor dulled by it. To the chagrin of many nobles, this increasingly unkempt-looking unit marched directly behind the Crown Prince's entourage, because this unit—holding a contract directly from the Crown—ranked equal in standing with any other that had contracted directly with the Crown, and the Crown Prince himself had dictated the order of march of those units.

It was ridiculous, and many of the nobles or their sons had mentioned—with delicate courtesy—to the Crown Prince that it was perhaps injudicious to so honor a foreigner, a mere mercenary. "If I'd known you wanted a mercenary unit, I could have hired you one," Duke Verrakai had said. "No need to deal with him yourself."

Young Marrakai, his father's Kirgan, had said as much to the younger prince, two steps farther from the throne. "Any of us could have hired him."

"Yes, but Gerry wanted to."

"But why?"

"I have no idea. I asked and he told me to figure it out for myself. The commander's a bastard, no doubt of that—no family anyone heard of anywhere."

"Any history at all?"

"Was in Halveric Company—"

"Ahhh. Lyonya, then. A bastard from *that* family?"

"I heard it was not, but you know—bastards. Some people don't claim them." That with a sniff. The royal family of Tsaia— Mahierans—acknowledged theirs, which made it fashionable to do so and less fashionable—honorable, they would say—not to do so. Kirgan Marrakai had often wondered if his father had sired any, but was afraid to ask, given the lectures he'd received as he grew into the ability.

"And yes, Gerry spent a campaign season studying something military with them down in Aarenis a few years ago, but that doesn't explain it, really."

It didn't explain anything, Kirgan Marrakai thought. As Kirgan, his father's heir, he could attend the daily briefings. His father, Duke Marrakai, had a seat at the table with the other senior nobles, the lesser barons standing behind them, while he and other kirgans stood silent, backs against the canvas walls of the large tent, supposedly learning something from watching their elders give way to the Prince and this stranger, this *mere* Captain Phelan, who had the Prince's ear when it came to matters military.

Well, he was a professional, after all. A hireling soldier fought for money: not honor, not loyalty. Rumor, gleaned from servants, was that the man had squired for Aliam Halveric in Aarenis, that he had attended the Falkian equivalent of the Bells. But he displayed no ruby such as Knights of Falk wore. Had he dropped out? Been thrown out? Had Halveric refused to hire him?

Arrogant young cock, thought Kirgan Marrakai, seeing the back of the man's head tilt toward the Crown Prince. And nothing to be proud about. Couldn't even keep a horse. Probably rode as badly as any farmer's brat. He amused himself that afternoon, imagining how his own stallion, who regularly threw him, would throw this arrogant young cock faster and harder.

The army moved slowly, leaving plenty of time for the young men of noble families to amuse themselves with sport: hunting and arms practice and mounted competitions. They had servants to set up and take down their tents, cook their meals, care for their horses and their clothes. They were—barring the arms practice all their fathers insisted on—on holiday. When they came to a tributary of the great river behind them, the army paused for two days to water the stock and the people, and servants went to washing clothes. The younger men found places for water play.

Kirgan Marrakai noticed that Captain Phelan let his men bathe but did not bathe with them. Arrogant, he told himself. *He* bathed every day from a tub in his father's tent, water brought in by his father's servants, the proper way to bathe. He told his friends.

They noticed the red-headed captain—hard to miss that flaming hair unhelmeted in the sun—heading still farther upstream, with a rag of some sort over his shoulder. Too shy to bathe with his men? Well. It would be good sport to know why. Maybe he... lacked something. They sniggered over that delicate suggestion. Maybe he was disfigured in some way not visible when he was covered neck to wrist and head to heel in cloth and leather or metal. Perhaps he was a branded criminal and the Crown Prince would definitely need to know *that*.

They turned aside, walked fifteen strides back toward the army, and then back around. He was out of sight; the stream there ran between taller banks than the rest, and they headed that way, but at a distance, sure he could not see them, moving as quietly as dozen young men with no training could.

One of them would go ahead, bending low, then taking quick looks, until he could see the red head and if it was moving, then signal the others. Finally, their forward scout waved them down and forward, and they came crawling through the lush grass to where they could see a wider space of moving water. And their target.

He was wet, naked but for boots, and armed, already out of the water, partway to them, sword in one hand, dagger in the other. His clothes lay on the grass at the water's edge; he had stamped back into his boots without their hearing or seeing him do it. He stopped when they rose from the grass, some of them already turning to flee. Kirgan Marrakai frankly stared; the man's pale skin was finely striped with white scars, perfectly aligned, overlain by later scars clearly from war-wounds: larger, more irregular, one or two still colored darker. And yet the body itself—he had never seen such perfect balance of muscle and bone and sinew. Or such a perfect mask of indifference to his situation: naked and alone before wealthy men clothed.

Then he grinned. "Oh, come, gentlemen, as I suppose you to be. Sons of nobility. Surely, *all* of you are not afraid of one man, even if he holds a sword! Draw yours, if you would feel more comfortable, while I go and dress. If you want to enjoy the water, I am through bathing, and the pool has been refreshed by the river's flow; it will not taint your…purity. And it is a perfect coolness today, refreshing without biting."

Every syllable etched as finely as any courtier's, with a precise fraction of indulgence, courtesy, scorn, and humor; Kirgan Marrakai felt striped by it, as the captain's body by whatever had scarred it so. He felt his face heat with a telltale flush, and his friends, he saw, felt the same. Damn the fellow! And then the fellow turned his back on them, heedless of their reaction, and walked back to his clothes. There on his back, the same pattern of fine scars as on his front, and on one firm buttock, what could only be a brand. Not a criminal's brand but a slave's.

Horror forced the indrawn breath he heard from all of them. The man shrugged, pulling on a shirt, toeing off his boots, carefully holding his sword in one armpit and dagger in the other, while pulling up his trousers, his socks, fastening the belt on which hung the scabbard, and sliding his weapons home, stamping back into his boots, then turning around.

"So, then: have you seen enough? Is your understanding *now* complete? Because if you want to see anything else—"

What else could there be? What other horrors? Kirgan Marrakai felt sick, and saw that Kirgan Serrostin, his closest friend, was faintly green around the lips. Had he actually thought of what else there could be?

"—Then we must come to blades," the captain said. "I think we would all benefit by not doing so, do you not?"

None of them had drawn a blade. None of them wanted to draw a blade now. They all, knowing each other well, had the certainty of nervous cattle that what they all wanted was to get back to the army, their safe herd, and never speak of it again, at least to anyone else. Maybe someday, when two or three were alone together…but not now.

He gave them a long, level stare out of grey eyes feral as a

wolf's. Then a sharp nod. "Good. We understand one another.
I am returning to my unit. Please do not follow me closely. You
may go ahead, or aside, as you please, of course, but I really can
commend the quality of the bathwater here."

As he came up the rise, they parted, as for a prince, and when
he had gone by, they did not turn to watch but stared at the
ground awhile. No one wanted to bathe there. Kirgan Marrakai
wondered if he would ever be able to strip off in front of his
father's body servant—or anyone else—again.

Inside his clothes, his body felt alien to him, wrong in some
way. He knew it wasn't flabby or misshapen, but he felt ashamed
even so. It was days before he realized what it lacked. Scars. The
experience those scars proved.

They came back to the camp slowly, reluctantly. Would the
captain have reported their spying on him? There was nothing
wrong with seeing another man bathing naked in a stream…they
had played in streams and ponds naked before. But they knew—
and knew they had known when they did it—that sneaking after
someone, some particular person, to peer at his nakedness, hoping to see something laughable or disgusting, was different. Not
honorable. The Crown Prince would not, they knew, approve.
Their own fathers would not approve. They could not approve
themselves, or each other, and each one sought for another to
blame. Kirgan Marrakai saw them glance at him and look away—
he was the one who had told them about the captain.

* * *

Though Kieri Phelan, captain of Fox Company, was confident he had behaved well in the matter of raw youths spying on
his bath—and just as glad it had not been a murderous attack by
Pargunese soldiers—he was not at all sure the youths had really

understood the magnitude of their error or his reaction to it. Of equal interest, a youth he would have expected to be with them…had not been.

Duke Verrakai's kirgan, usually one of that group in the commanders' tent…usually, in fact, standing next to Kirgan Marrakai and Kirgan Serrostin, sometimes between them…had not been with them. Duke Verrakai and Duke Marrakai appeared to occupy a secondary level below that of Duke Mahieran, and slightly above Dukes Serrostin and Elloran.

A mercenary commander, Aliam had told him, *must know as much or more about the power structure of employers as the employer knows about the commander. You've met a prince of Tsaia, a future king, and he's mentioned offering you a contract? Pay close attention whenever you see him among his nobles.* So Kieri had, and knew that Verrakai and Marrakai were rivals, and not friendly ones. That Serrostin and Marrakai were friends, Elloran was afraid of Verrakai. That Kirgan Verrakai, whose father was not friends with Kirgan Marrakai's father, had been cultivating Kirgan Marrakai for some purpose not yet clear, and yet…he had not taken part in yesterday's hunt. Had the others told him? Deliberately not invited him? Or had he chosen not to go for reasons of his own?

He puzzled over this and the currents of ambition that swirled among the older men, not just the dukes but the counts and barons. The nobles were not skilled at war of the type he himself knew best, but quite skilled at the methods of courtly intrigue, wielding small units of influence as skillfully as a man might use a dagger to penetrate the weak points in armor. As in fighting physically, some were more direct and others more apt at ruse and guile.

Verrakai was certainly that kind. For himself, he knew Verrakai deeply resented his having a direct contract. Verrakai's attempts to discredit the upstart mercenary were not so obvious as to catch the prince's attention—always courteous, always mild, little corrections that weren't, seeming deference to Kieri's practical experience but with little suggestions and questions that hinted at his concern that Kieri—so young for such expertise but of course mentored by the famous Halverics—might not quite measure up to the task they laid on him. Under those constant barbs, Kieri sensed both hostility and more military knowledge than most. He found the man annoying, but he found many non-soldiers annoying. A risk of his experience, Aliam had said. Now he wondered if Verrakai and his kirgan were part of a coordinated attack…but on what? The Marrakai family as a whole? Or more? Even the Crown?

* * *

The next day, marching once more at the head of his company, dusty, unable to see farther than the Crown Prince's entourage ahead of him, he was caught between annoyance and amusement at himself. Who did he think he was, indeed—as he'd heard others say—he who did not know, could not name, either of his parents, or his place of birth, or anything remotely respectable in his past until his arrival at Aliam Halveric's home as a starveling. How could any of these people respect, let alone admire him?

Yet there he was, with an independent contract, and the promise of a chance to earn—in good time—a grant of land. He had seen it, even.

"Go take a look," the prince had said. "It's empty, cold, near-barren. But it's the largest area in my father's realm not already occupied, or at least claimed. No one has wanted it. No fields, no orchards, no towns: barren, some say, and too much work, say others. Yet it is my father's, and I would see it useful and well governed. Go see."

And he had borrowed a horse—after the horse-master had checked with the Crown Prince yet again and given him, he was sure, the worst horse in the royal stables, gray about the muzzle and eyes, with splints in both forelegs and a hitch of some kind in the off hock. He had ridden, at a pace that let the old horse loosen up and enjoy the trip, day after day through forest and hills, until on a wet day the view had opened to a broad plain with hills off to either side, a brisk little river that might, some-day, run a mill. Hills on three sides, then, and a wide, presently soggy plain rising slightly to the north, where it disappeared into a dank mist.

His mind produced an image of the mill on the river, near a town...here. A bridge over the river, wide enough for wagons to carry supplies and troops to march, there. Another town over to the west—out of sight except in his mind. He rode out across the stream, onto the soggy plain. Even this early in the year, it had grass the old horse was glad to eat. And ample room for any number of troops to drill. He could see it all: a big walled fort to guard the land and the track that would in time become a real road south to Vérella. His mind built it quickly into what it could be. A base for protection and for training.

Aliam's home was crowded between a mountain and the dense Lyonyan forest of elventaig, closed to humans: this would be open. Colder, yes, but then his troops would be fit to fight Pargun to the east in those hills, hold off the horse nomads to the north, if any threatened. His horse's hoofprints and the grass showed that the land was fertile enough for grain. And in the shelter of the hills the towns could have walled gardens and fruit orchards.

He rode back to Vérella, treating the old horse so carefully, the horsemaster was amazed at the difference in the animal. "He's not limping at all—what did you do? What poultice? A special herb?"

"No, just careful riding, never fast and not too long at one time. He's a good fellow, this one." He patted the horse and it rubbed its head on him.

And so, the offer of a chance at a land grant had become a promise of one…in good time, which meant at the Crown's convenience. But at least it would not be given away, he was assured.

Reason enough to keep his temper with those boys and their arrogance, reason enough to keep a smooth tongue to all. Aliam would be happy with him, if he knew, but he was not minded to write Aliam about it, not until the grant was actually his. Still, the dust was annoying, and he did wish the nobility would not make it worse by galloping past him every time they wanted to come to or leave the Crown Prince's presence. If he'd had a horse—he'd sold his along with all the other gifts Aliam had given him to outfit his troops for this very mission—he could have seen over some of this dust.

So, when he heard the rapid hoofbeats coming up from behind, and the voice yelling at the horse, followed by a dust-blurred sight of the horse bucking along and the rider finally being launched, he knew both who it was and what had happened. The Marrakai were known for breeding good horses, but this kirgan was not, Kieri thought, a good horseman. The horse was, obviously, both young and difficult, a red stallion with one white foot that had traveled hollow-backed and crooked every time Kieri had seen it pass. He'd seen the young man launched before, and noticed the same pattern every time.

Except that this time, the horse ran toward his unit, and Kieri caught the trailing rein. One problem was obvious and he reached out to fix it.

"Let go of my horse, you—!" The young man stumbled toward him.

"I'm but settling him," Kieri said, in as easy a voice as he owned. "The curb chain wasn't adjusted correctly."

"What do you know about curb chains?! You don't even have a horse." The young man was angry, having been launched right in front of everyone clustered around the prince.

"I have had," Kieri said, unhooking the chain, giving it a twist, and hooking it again with the chain flat and the hook pointed away from the horse. The horse bumped him with its nose. Most horses liked him, he'd found out at Aliam's.

"I suppose you think you can ride better than I do!" Still angry, still not thinking, was Kieri's analysis, and he saw other faces turned to this conversation. Oh, well, sometimes truth hurt.

"I can ride; I do not judge myself an expert."

"Well, I am," the youth said, just as loud, and having come near enough, he grabbed the opposite rein and yanked hard. The horse threw up its head, half-reared, and bumped the youth with its shoulder. He lost his grip and went down again.

"YOU did that!" he said, even louder, reaching for his sword.

This was not, Kieri told himself, going to end well, whatever he did. He flipped the reins over the horse's head, and his sergeant ran up and took them, clearing space. Kieri rocked just a bit, heel to toe, finding his best balance on this uneven surface but not moving to draw. Four inches of steel showed above the boy's scabbard. But out of the dust another voice intervened.

"Kirgan Marrakai! Do I see you drawing on one of my commanders? Stand where you are, sir." Voices rose.

"Silence." Then, to someone else, the Prince said, "Tell Duke Marrakai I would speak with him." A man ran off to the side. The entire procession had stopped by now; the dust settled slowly. Kieri looked at the Prince, who looked back at him and nodded at Kieri's empty hands. "Is the horse hurt, Captain?"

"No, my lord prince."

"Good. Did I hear you correctly, there was an error of adjustment of the bit?"

"The curb chain, my lord prince. It had not been twisted quite flat, and the hook pointed inward."

"Anything else?"

"If it were my horse, I would check the saddle adjustment; it seemed to me that it had perhaps slipped a bit to one side while being girthed. But the dust could have obscured my view, and it was bucking."

Duke Marrakai rode up. "My lord prince."

"Yes, I wish your opinion."

The Duke's gaze shifted from his son to the Prince, Kieri, the horse, and back to the Prince. "Yes, my lord."

"Who is at fault if a horse is bitted incorrectly, perhaps not girthed correctly, and bucks in consequence?"

"The rider," the Duke said promptly.

"Even if a groom tacks it up for the rider?"

"Yes, my lord, always. The rider must check everything before mounting. May I ask what happened?"

"You know your son's horse bucks frequently?"

"Yes. It is young. I advised him to bring a more experienced mount, but he insisted on bringing this one."

"If it is shown that someone else, someone who adjusted or adjusts the tack, can ride the horse the rest of the morning without it bucking...what would you think?"

The Duke scowled at his son. "I would think the rider—in this case my son—had been negligent in checking his tack."

"And what would you do?"

"I could send him home," the Duke offered.

"And what good would that do for the horse?" the Crown Prince asked the sky, and then went on without giving the Duke time to answer. "I tell you what, Duke Marrakai: if you will allow, I will set this rider's punishment myself. First, we shall see to the matter of negligence. Captain, bring the horse here. Duke, you and I will inspect the tack."

The horse walked over calmly as Kieri led it. At the Crown Prince's prompt, he pointed to the curb chain, which they agreed was correct, and then put it back in the position he'd found it. They nodded, then Kieri put it back correctly.

"The saddle?"

"May I take it off completely?"

"Of course."

Kieri showed the underside of the saddle, to all appearances normal for a Tsaian war saddle. But Duke Marrakai frowned and turned to his son. "That's not Gill's saddle, is it?"

"No, sir. His was being re-flocked and the groom said this one, Blink's saddle, would fit well enough."

Kieri laid the saddle on the horse's bare back and felt under it. "It's wide enough and not too wide…this side has fair contact, no lumps." He went to the off side. "It's… My lord Duke, would you feel this?"

The Duke ran his hand between horse and saddle. "Well. Take it off; I'll feel his back." Kieri took the saddle down again, then moved behind the horse to look along the spine. He could see what he'd felt. Uneven muscle development behind the shoulder meant the saddle would pinch there where it did not on the near side. "That's why his own saddle was being re-stuffed," the Duke said. "And that—and the curb—is why he started bucking."

"If there is a saddler with the army," Kieri said, "he should be able to re-stuff this today and then adjust after a ride."

The Crown Prince looked at him. "My saddler is with us. But you, could you ride him as it is now?"

"I could, but it would be uncomfortable for the horse. I can sit differently, take some of the pressure off, but not all."

"Try. A few minutes only; I want to see and so does the Duke." A sharp glance aimed at the Duke, who nodded.

Kieri saddled, accepted a leg up from his sergeant, and picked up the reins. The stallion came up into his hand, flexing correctly; he could feel the horse react calmly to a different seat. Walk, easy. Trot, no shaking head, no hollow back. Turn this way, turn that, halt, back.

"A short canter only, heart lead, I think," said the Duke. Kieri nodded, asked for it from walk, and the horse bent to it and bounded off correctly in the first stride, bent away from the side that needed a little more room. But its ears had stiffened, Kieri noticed. "Who taught you riding?" the Duke asked.

"Aliam Halveric's horsemaster and Aliam himself, when I was his squire," Kieri said. "And then, in Falk's Hall, we learned saddle fitting and bitting as well as advanced riding."

"Such as?"

Kieri named the figures they'd been taught. "But this fellow needs more training before he's ready for that."

"Agreed." Duke Marrakai turned to the Prince. "I yield to your judgment, my lord prince."

"Well, Kirgan," the Prince said, turning to the boy, standing pale and miserable before them. "This man you do not respect rode your horse better than you do, and with more concern for the horse. What do you say for yourself?'

"I was wrong." The voice sounded even younger, choked with

emotion. "I—I trusted others and should have trusted my father first, to know I needed an older, quieter horse."

"Well, then, I have a plan for you, so you do not waste your opportunity to learn. You will not ride your horse for five days, during which its saddle will be re-stuffed and adjusted until the saddler's satisfied, and during which you will walk with Captain Phelan's cohort. You will watch the saddler do the re-stuffing, and he and Captain Phelan will instruct you in saddle fitting. You will observe how Captain Phelan handles the horse, how he tacks it up, how he cares for it, and you will take over from him when he permits. You will then—until we are within a league of the Pargunese border—listen and learn from him what you may be doing as a rider that makes the horse uneasy. It is my command that Captain Phelan report to me and to your father any errors you make that may injure this or other horses, and by the time we reach Pargun, you should be far advanced in your horsemanship. Do you agree?"

What was there for a boy to say but what he said? "Yes, my lord prince."

The Prince nodded and turned away; Duke Marrakai moved with him.

Kieri knew that despite the acquiescence, the boy was boiling with indignation: he had been humiliated in front of everyone by his horse, Kieri, the prince, his own father, and he was in no state to think clearly. "Do you have a halter or lead for this horse, so we can take him to the saddler?"

"In my father's wagon," the boy said shortly.

"I don't know which it is," Kieri said. Ahead of him, the Prince's wagon lurched into motion, and he turned to his sergeant. "Sergeant, take over for the moment. The Prince has ordered we get this horse to the saddler."

"Captain." Siger's face was as blank as his own, he saw. They were all on bog ground until they got the boy and the horse both sorted out. One wrong step and they could be in it to the neck. And no grant of land. And a boy mired in helpless anger, and a horse mired in bad training, bad riding, bad saddle fitting. He understood now, though he still wished it to have been different, Aliam's refusal to hire him as a junior captain. He pushed that aside and looked at the boy again. "Can you take me to it, either your father's supply wagon with horse tack in it or the Prince's saddler?"

"They're both with the other horse-supply wagons," Kirgan Marrakai said, with slightly less stiffness. "Back this way." They walked toward the tail of the line, the horse snatching now and then at grass.

"How old is he?" Kieri asked. "Five? Six?"

"Five. He was backed last year by the trainer."

"Still quite young, then."

"Yes. The trainer let me sit on him last year, because I was so light. Then I grew, but he was a year older and also grew two fingers, so I thought—I thought I was doing well."

"You grew taller; did your trainer explain what that does to your seat?"

"Taller? I thought only heavier mattered. That's all the trainer talked about, how young horses should never carry too much weight."

"That's so, but when boys grow into men, they change their shape, where the weight is, as well as how much. Where you can put your leg on a horse, how your balance changes when your shoulders broaden. When did you start drilling with the sword you carry instead of a boy's shorter one?"

"Last winter; it was a Midwinter gift."

"And have you done mounted exercises with it? Knocking rag balls off poles?"

"Yes."

"So, you have more weight in your sword arm, and as you reach out to do that, more weight shifts onto that side of the saddle, and your horse tries to hold steady—and one side needs more strength than the other, so his back developed unevenly in the past few months."

The boy stopped short. "I—I never thought of that! The riding master never mentioned that!"

"But still not strong enough, and doesn't feel good where the saddle pinches, so he hollows, to avoid the pressure—"

"Yes! I know he does, and when I try to make him lift his back, he bucks." He looked at Kieri wide-eyed. "How do you know that? Why doesn't our riding master? He just says, 'More leg, more leg, ride him into the bit.'"

"Did he tell you to wear spurs?"

"Yes. Because my legs aren't strong enough, he said."

"There are ways to strengthen legs, if you care to try."

"You don't have spurs."

"I did. I sold them."

"Because you don't use them?"

"No, because I needed the money for something else."

"What?"

"It's a long story. How much farther, do you think, and which will be first, your father's wagon or the saddler's?"

"The saddler's. Well, the Prince's wagons of horse feed, tack, and his grooms and saddler will be there. See that pennant? That's the royal one, so it's one of those."

The saddler, when they found him, had spare halters; they borrowed one. Then he went to work quickly, explaining to

Kieri—and Kirgan Marrakai, when reminded that this was the Kirgan's horse—what needed to be done and why, and what exercises might help even out the muscling of the horse's back. Kieri and his student, as he now thought of the boy, walked along behind the saddler's wagon with the horse, now tied to the tailboard, while the saddler worked in his shop, built into the wagon.

The boy now seemed less angry and fragile than he had earlier. "Why is he using different colors of wool?"

"Let's ask him," Kieri said. "You or me?"

"*Me* ask?"

"Surely. You want to know; I'd like to know. You can do it."

The boy did ask, and the saddler explained, even handing the boy small tufts of wool to feel: the dark, the light, the softest, the springiest. Several times the saddle went on and came back off the horse, then the saddler said, "Now, Kirgan, time you get up and let me see how it compresses as you ride."

The boy looked sideways at Kieri. "If you don't mind," Kieri said to the saddler. "I'm a little heavier and will compress it faster."

"Oh." The saddler looked back and forth at them.

"It's all right," the boy said. "My father wants him to ride Gill for a while anyway."

"Ah. Well, then." He offered Kieri a leg up and then walked beside the horse, feeling under the saddle as the horse walked along, seemingly quite calm. "Like you to give him a bit of trot and canter," the saddler said, and unfastened the halter. Kieri turned the horse out of the line of wagons and trotted him in circles both directions, then cantered, then a hand gallop both ways. The saddler checked again, made one more adjustment, then nodded. "Should be good for today. Bring him back to me tomorrow, after he's ridden, or any time he kicks up again."

"We've a walk to catch up with my group," Kieri said. "To

keep our senior commander happy, I'd best ride the horse, but you can tail or use the stirrup leather if you like."

"Tail?"

"Have you never? When you have reason to move faster than walking is comfortable, and not enough horses for all, a horse can carry a light rider, and help along two more at least." He slid one foot out of the stirrup. "Put your hand there, and see. He will walk faster than either of us would want to. If you were taller, you could hold on to the stirrup leather; right now, it would make your shoulder sore. You can also, going uphill, catch the tail and let one pull you along. They won't kick if the tail's being pulled straight back smoothly, not jerking. It doesn't hurt them."

The boy did that, and they passed wagon after wagon, until Kieri saw his troops again, and the prince's wagons just ahead. They slowed to match them, and Kieri said, "It's our secret, eh? If anyone asks, you're just good at walking fast," When the boy pulled his hand free, he set his own foot back in the stirrup. "I suspect many of your friends don't know about the kinds of wool the saddlers use," he added. "Now you know some new things. Here's another. Come meet my sergeant. He used to be in Halveric Company in Aarenis and Lyonya."

Over the next few days, the boy asked question after question, mostly reasonable ones, as if he'd been told before that asking questions was unsuitable. Kieri and Siger—and several of the troops—answered as if he were any new recruit or squire.

Kieri, remembering himself with Aliam—at first afraid to ask anything and then, in a flood, asking questions all day long and into the night—found the boy far less arrogant than he'd thought earlier. The boy was quick to take suggestions, showing up the fourth morning in mail shirt and breast-and-back after Siger had told him wearing armor would help strengthen his legs. Why had he been so touchy before? Had it been the other boys, or something else?

* * *

One evening, coming out of the daily conference, Duke Marrakai asked Kieri to walk with him. "The lad's different. I thought he'd sulk and complain, and you have him smiling and cheerful."

"He's a good boy," Kieri said.

"Sometimes," the Duke said. "And sometimes, I've wanted to put a knot on his head. You have no children yet, do you?"

"No, but I watched Aliam Halveric and his wife with theirs, and I remember them with me. I ignored your lad's sulks and treated him as a sensible person, which he's turned out to be. I'm going to put him back on his horse tomorrow."

"Well. You should have a horse. You ride very well and you know horses. And, apparently, boys."

"I will have a horse again someday. I want one of your breeding. Your son's horse is the best I've ridden. Aliam had a halfbred of yours. Tell me, what do you charge for the fullbred colts?"

The Duke looked at him squarely. "They don't come cheap."

"No good horse does but by accident. I will have one someday, and now you know it will be treated well."

"Indeed. The Prince says he's thinking of giving you that barren mess up north as a grant if you do well in this campaign and another one or two. No one else has wanted it, at any price or reward."

"It would suit me," Kieri said. "In time it would thrive, with good management. Hard at the start, of course, but are not the best horses often those difficult to train well early on?"

"You are not afraid of challenges."

Kieri laughed. "No, my lord, I am not. Challenges come to

all, early and late; Aliam taught me that the measure of men is how they meet them. Let me have raw land, or a young horse—"

"Or a young boy?"

"I cannot speak of your son in such terms; he is yours, and a future Duke of Tsaia."

"Well. I see him as a challenge; he has been for me. And I like what I see, Captain. Teach him to ride better, and care for horses better, and we shall be friends a long time."

"If you knew Aliam, my lord, he would tell you tales about me at your son's age that would curl not only your hair but your horse's tail. If I am able to help him through this, I am happy to do so."

Later that evening, the boy said, "We should not have done what we did. *I* should not have done what I did." None of the boys had spoken to Kieri about it before, but there was no doubt what the boy meant.

"You're right," Kieri said matter-of-factly, setting the stallion's saddle on its rack. "But you did, and it's done, and you're not doing it now."

"No, but I needed to say that. I'm sorry I did it. I'm sorry I spied on you. I'm sorry…"

What would Aliam say to that? What had Aliam said to so many of his own unwitting cruelties, blunders, thoughtless deeds, including those that got men killed?

"Listen to me," Kieri said. "You did something you knew was wrong, and you know that some things cannot be undone. You can't forget what you saw, can you?"

The boy's head shook side to side; his eyes glistened.

"So, when I was your age, and Aliam Halveric's squire, I did things I knew I should not do, and some of those things could not be undone. Men died, for some of my mistakes. Yours harmed no one but yourself. To be good men, when we are grown, we must learn to think. Beyond what feels good, beyond what feels like fun, beyond what feels like it will win us advantage: we must learn to look ahead and think. And it's hard. You have learned important things in these days: about your horse, about me, about yourself. Now you know you *can* learn. And I know you *will* learn."

"Will I make more mistakes?"

"Oh, yes. But not the same one. If you're like me, you will make mistakes over and over. Everyone does. It's how we learn. When you started riding, you fell off a lot, didn't you?"

"Yes."

"And now you ride confidently at all gaits but bucking—anyone can be bucked off. So, as you move into adulthood, you will make fewer mistakes but not none, and when you don't make any mistakes at all, you'll have made the worst, because you'll have quit learning. Keep learning, keep failing, but learn from the mistake, correct it, don't repeat it." He grinned. "That's what Aliam taught me; I didn't learn it by myself."

"I don't think I'm ready to ride my horse again."

"Why not?"

A mischievous grin this time. "Because I'm still making mistakes here. Because my horse shouldn't suffer for them. Teach me to ride your way, please, and show me by riding him yourself."

"Now, *that* will require your father's permission: who's going to ask him?" Kieri grinned back at him.

"I will," the boy said, with no hesitation. "I will, and he will say yes, and then he'll tell me he told me the horse was too much for me in this situation, and I'll say he was right, and then he'll say I can ride his old horse, his second. We can ride together."

The End

Elizabeth Moon, a Texas native, is a Marine Corps veteran with degrees in history and biology. She began writing stories in childhood but did not make her first fiction sale until age forty. She has published twenty-eight novels, including Nebula Award winner *The Speed of Dark*, Hugo Award finalist *Remnant Population*, four short-fiction collections including *Moon Flights* in 2007, and over fifty short-fiction pieces in anthologies and magazines.

THE

TENTH ANNIVERSARY EDITION

SPEED

ELIZABETH MOON

WITH A NEW INTRODUCTION BY THE AUTHOR

OF

DARK

A Novel

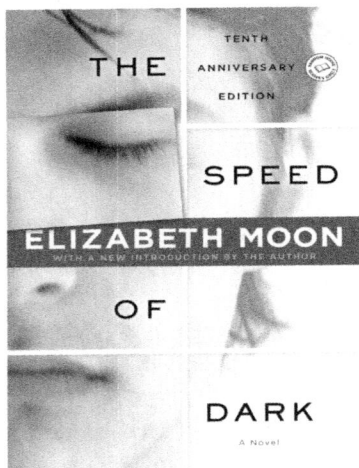

**Winner
2003 Nebula Award
for Best Novel**

**Finalist
Arthur C. Clarke Prize
for Best Novel**

Perfect for your next book club selection

In 2004, The Speed of Dark was selected for Kansas City's "United We Read" initiative. Since then, it has been used for campus reading events at Ohio State University, Clemson University, and Suny Oswego. It has also been a part of community events for library systems in Howard County, Massachusetts, and Georgetown, Texas.

This book is part of the Random House Reader's Circle collection and comes with a discussion guide that makes it the perfect choice for any reading group.

"Inevitably, *The Speed of Dark* has been compared to Daniel Keyes' classic and tragic Flowers for Algernon, in which a mentally disabled young man is medically enhanced to become a genius. *The Speed of Dark* may be an even greater book...; it is [a] subtle, eerily nuanced character portrait of a man who is both unforgettable and unlike anyone else in fiction ... It is a measure of Elizabeth Moon's genius that she enables a reader to thoroughly experience the world through Lou's tangled but exhilarating neurology, and wonder what we "normal" people are missing when we don't acknowledge our connection to those who seem so different from us. A lot of novels promise to change the way a reader sees the world; *The Speed of Dark* actually does."
— Elizabeth Hand,
Washington Post Book World

"A touching account. Well-written, intelligent, quite moving. Moon places the reader inside the world of an autistic and unflinchingly conveys the authenticity of his situation."
— *Kirkus*, starred review

FOR NEWS ABOUT JABBERWOCKY BOOKS AND AUTHORS

Sign up for our newsletter*: http://eepurl.com/b84tDz
visit our website: awfulagent.com/ebooks
or follow us on twitter: @awfulagent

THANKS FOR READING!

*We will never sell or give away your email address, nor use it for nefarious purposes.

Printed in Dunstable, United Kingdom